ARCADIA

Published by Pugnacious Publishing

ACARDIA

GUY PORTMAN

ONE

I HAVE JUST GOT OFF THE PLANE. The flight took eight hours and fifty-one minutes. A baby in the row behind me screamed for half the time. Even with earphones in, I could hear it. Mum twists her head around and says, 'Come on.'

I pull my wheeled suitcase over to her. Ahead of us in the arrivals queue are two families and an old couple. On the wall to my right is a billboard with a sandy beach on it, blue sea, and *Welcome to Antigua*. I am going to be living here for a while. Mum didn't specify how long. *We'll see,* she said, *depends how it goes. Probably a year.* She wanted a break from London is why we're here. Mum's father's family are from Antigua. At the top of the escalator we came down, I can hear Caribbean music being played on an electronic keyboard. Three places behind me in the queue, there is a young woman with long, silky blonde hair just like Serena's, my sort of girlfriend in London.

'What're you doing?' Mum is dragging her suitcase over to one of the immigration booths. I stop looking at the girl. 'Hurry up!'

I follow her to the booth. The female immigration officer takes our passports and asks lots of questions. She returns our passports and we collect our other bags from the baggage reclaim. On the other side of the terminal's glass doors, I can see her father. Mum shrieks, waves her left hand about in the air, rushes out of the building, and throws her arms around his neck. I drag my suitcase over to them. It's hot and humid out here. Mum releases her grip on her father's neck and stares at me.

'Say hello to your grandfather.'

Her father is grinning at me. Haven't seen him in seven years, or more. He has a white beard, is tall, and looks strong for an old person.

'Horatio! Welcome to Antigua.'

'Hello.'

He slaps me on the shoulder, and says, 'You're all grown up.' We go to his white Toyota Corolla. It has a big dent on one side. Mum gets in the front, her father puts the suitcases in the boot, and we drive off. Near the airport there is a cricket ground, which he tells me the Chinese built. Mum says, 'Horatio likes playing cricket. He sometimes plays with his sister in the garden at home.'

That is not cricket, it's just hitting a ball with a bat. He says, 'How is Shaneeka getting on at college?'

'Doing really well there. Going to miss her so much.'

'Of course, darling.' Her father takes his hand off the gear stick and strokes her arm. 'Missed you and your sister all the time when I moved back here.'

There are roadworks and the traffic is moving at jogging speed. Mum and her father are talking non-stop. The last time I came to Antigua I was eight. Now I am fifteen. Mum's father's house isn't far from the capital St. John's where the airport is. Nowhere is that far from the capital – Antigua is small, only one hundred and eight square miles. The house is halfway up this hill, and the track up to it is full of holes and bumpy. We stop outside a gate with balloons tied to its posts. He opens the gate. Mum's family are in the courtyard.

Mum throws herself out of the car, runs into the courtyard and hugs them. There are four of them. There is an old woman, Mum's stepmother. Bossy, I remember. There is a gigantic man with a shaved head, who I think is the stepmother's son. And a small child, a girl. No idea who she is. At the back of the group is

2

Cousin Dougal. He is three years older than me and has stumpy dreadlocks. They have these land crabs here. When I came to Antigua last time it was New Year's and there were firecrackers in the house. We gave them to the crabs. They clutched onto them, they exploded, and the crabs blew into bits. It was over there on my right where we did it, on the waste ground between Mum's father's house and the next property down.

Everyone is looking this way. Mum stomps over to the car. When I clamber out, she grabs me by the elbow and says through the side of her mouth, 'What the hell are you playing at? Told you to be on your best behaviour here. This isn't a good start.'

She pushes me into the courtyard. Her father's wife says, 'Welcome Horatio. My how you've grown.'

'Hello.'

'This is my son Carlton. He was working in The States when you came here all those years ago.'

He shakes my hand firmly, and says, 'Welcome to Antigua.' The little girl is clutching onto one of his massive legs and peering up at me. 'My five-year-old daughter, Gloria.'

She waves at me, and says, 'Hi.'

'Hello.'

Cousin Dougal comes over, bumps my fist against his, and says, 'Wa gwaan?' *What does that mean?* 'What's up? What's going on?'

I shrug my shoulders and say, 'Just arrived in Antigua.'

He smirks and says, 'Alright?'

Mum's father carries her luggage to the building on the right side of the yard. I take mine. It's a mini house with a kitchenette and living room downstairs, and two bedrooms with ensuite bathrooms upstairs. My bedroom is a reasonable size, has aircon and a tiny balcony. Stayed in this room last time. This is where Mum and I will be living. Her father and stepmother live in the slightly bigger house on the other side of the courtyard. I am planning to relax in my room, as I'm quite tired after the flight.

3

But then Mum's father announces that we are all going to the beach to see the sunset, and we best get moving or we'll miss it. I travel there in a jeep with Dougal, Carlton, and his daughter.

I am standing barefoot in the warm sand, looking at the sea. Waves are lapping on the beach, the sky on the horizon has turned bright orange, and the sun is so low it is almost touching the water. Two large birds flapping above the sea are silhouetted against the sun.

'Look Horatio!' shrieks Mum. 'Pelicans.' I see them. The sun drops into the sea. 'Wow, it's so beautiful, so resplendent.' The orange light on the horizon begins to dim. Mum wraps her arm around my shoulders. 'Antigua is a tropical island paradise; you'll love living here.'

TWO

THREE WEEKS LATER – I get off the bus and walk along the main road. A mangy dog with patchy fur trots past me. Either side of the road are rows of shacks with peeling paint and overgrown front yards with broken fences. On a shack's porch, an old man wearing tattered shorts is drinking from a beer can. I smell ganja. My destination is a one-storey wooden building with yellow walls, a brown roof, and no windows. The name of the place is scrawled on the wall at the front in red paint – *Bevis and Gene's Laundry*. Underneath it is the phone number and email address.

The business is named after Mum's father and his wife Genevieve. Guess her name was too long for the sign, so it was shortened. Mum's father also owns a couple of holiday homes and an auto repair shop that Carlton runs. On Saturdays I work here. Mum made me do it. She was encouraged to by her father and bossy stepmother. Mum said I have to make a contribution for my upkeep and that it's an opportunity for me to learn about work.

I get paid nine Eastern Caribbean Dollars an hour to work here, which is approximately two pounds seventy pence. Half is handed over to Mum. She isn't even working at the moment. She gets money from renting out our house in London. Says she will get a job soon but needs a break first. It is hot out here. With half of the washing and drying machines on most of the time, it will be eight to ten degrees warmer in there. My timing is perfect, it's nine on the dot. Punctuality is rare over here. When I go inside, the manager says, 'Good morning, Horatio.'

'Good morning.'

A couple of the machines are running and it's already hot. By late morning, it will be nearly forty degrees. There is aircon in the office, but in here there are only ceiling fans that blow hot air about. The manager shouts from the office, 'Horatio, delivery!'

There is a blue van parked on the kerb with its side door open. It will be bed linen from the Airbnbs up the road. When I go down to the van, the driver says, 'Wah gwaan? You good?'

'Hell no! It's Saturday and I'm working in a launderette.'

The driver laughs. He has very white teeth that contrast with his coal black face. I haul the three big blue linen bags from the back of the van, carry them into the laundrette, stuff the contents into machines, put detergent and softener in, and switch them on. The manager is holding a broom and a bin liner.

'Back yard needs sweeping.'

'I'm not doing it.'

She *huffs* and says, 'You work here; you do what I say. That's the job.'

'No way, sweeping isn't part of my job description. Laundry is what I do.'

She leans the broom against the wall, waddles into the office and closes the door …

It's now twelve-thirty, and I am sitting on the steps at the front of the laundrette, sipping from a can of Coca-Cola I got from a shack shop on the roadside. A group of girls are walking this way. One of them is Dalilah. She is slim, has caramel-coloured skin, big brown eyes, and curly brown hair cut quite short. I met her the first day I worked here when she stopped by to chat with the manager. Last Saturday, I spent my lunchbreak with her. Dalilah stops by the wall at the front of the launderette, waves at me, and says, '*Hi.*'

'Hello.'

She says something to the other girls and they walk off. Dalilah skips up to me – 'What's up?'

'On my break.'

'Walk with me for a bit.'

We walk up the track next to the launderette. Dalilah asks if I'm having a good day. I say, 'No! Been ramming dirty laundry into machines all morning in the searing heat.'

Dalilah giggles. She squeezes my elbow, and says, 'But it's looking up now, right?' I nod. 'How is island life treating you?'

'Good and bad.'

'Launderette is bad, maybe. Otherwise, it's alright, surely? It's not cold and raining all the time like the UK. Laid back here, not hectic …'

On the side of the track is a rusted car with no wheels. She lives further up the track, in a shanty, consisting of hemmed-in little wooden shacks. A teenager with braided stumpy dreadlocks wearing a dirty yellow T-shirt, is strolling along the track towards us. Dalilah *tuts*. It is the eighteen-year-old loser, Javel. He also lives in the shanty. The manager pointed him out to me the week before last and told me to avoid him as he's *bad news*. When he walks past us, he glares at me and spits on the ground. Dalilah *tuts* again. My break is over and it's time to get back to work. Dalilah kisses me on the cheek and skips off up the track. She stops, pivots around and blows me a kiss.

Three of the washing machines have completed their cycle. I haul everything out of them and shove it all in the drying machines. Stuff could be hung outside as it's sunny a lot of the time. Rains a fair bit too though, there's dust, and exhaust fumes from the road. The laundry wouldn't smell professionally cleaned that's for sure. Mum's father walks into the launderette. He's not grinning like he usually is.

'Horatio, take a seat.' I sit on the wooden bench that runs along the middle of the launderette. 'Sometimes we have to do things we don't want to. In the UK, I worked in drainage. Didn't want to do it much of the time, as it was dirty, wet and cold. But I did it anyway. All that hard work paid off eventually. See!' He extends an arm in the direction of the washing machines. 'That's how I was able to pay for all this … Too many people on this blessed island don't know the meaning of hard work. My grandson isn't going to be one of them. Now get out back and get sweeping.'

This sucks. I pick up the broom and a bin liner and exit the launderette. I see three boys, tourists about my age, walking along the road. They must be heading to the beach behind the trees on the other side of the road. How unfair. When I go around the side of the building, a rat dashes past me, scuttles off through the undergrowth and onto the track I was on with Dalilah. It smells of urine and there are mosquitos. No wonder the manager didn't want to clean here. There are paving stones with weeds growing around the sides of them, littered with spliff butts and empty beer cans. I start sweeping.

That looks like used toilet paper on the paving stone over there … It is used toilet paper. Smells rank and has flies circling it. I pick the toilet paper up with two sticks and drop it in the bin liner. Job done. Making my way to the entrance to the launderette when I see on the track a bright blue mustang. Belongs to a drug dealer who lives in the shanty up there. Dalilah told me about him. She says he is bad and sometimes bothers her.

*

08:23 – Monday morning – I get off the bus. On the pavement there is a man pushing a shopping trolley full of junk. His mouth is hanging open and he has matted dreadlocks that haven't been shampooed in forever. There are lots of homeless drug addicts around here. Two boys from my school passing by on either side of me, say, 'Good morning.'

They walk ahead of me up the hill, at the top of which is the cathedral. It was built in the nineteenth century and has two baroque-style towers. The cathedral has fallen into disrepair bigtime. Foliage is growing from the towers, the stonework is filthy and crumbling, and some of the windows have been boarded up. My new school is on the other side of the cathedral and a bit further down the hill. Antigua Boys High School has metal gates with barbed wire on top of them. Next to the gates is a sign – 'Drugs End All Dreams'. I go through the gates and into the small concrete yard. The three-storey red and yellow building is small for a school and there is not much in the way of facilities.

The first class of the day is maths. I go into the classroom, take the maths textbook from my mini rucksack, and put it on the desk along with a pen, a pad of A4 paper and a calculator. The teacher walks in and says, 'Good morning.'

Everyone stands up and says, 'Good morning, Sir.'

Everyone sits down. The teacher is an old guy who always wears a tweed jacket, however hot it is. He says, 'Today, we will be progressing with probability. Probability is always presented on a scale of zero to one.' *Like most of the teachers he speaks clear English, unlike lots of people over here.* 'Probabilities can be written in one of three ways. What are the three ways, Garfield?'

The boy at the desk on my left says, 'Fraction, decimals, percentages.'

'Correct … Venn diagrams show the logical relation between sets …'

Have come across Venn diagrams before and know that I am going to be good at them. This school doesn't even have a science lab, proper computer room, or art centre. And it's in the middle of a shithole. However, the boys here are well behaved, so it is easy to concentrate in class unlike my old school in London where there were idiots always trying to be funny and impress the others. The teacher is writing on the whiteboard at the front of the class. *Ninety classmates were asked whether they own a laptop or a tablet. Fifty-two own a laptop, forty-five own a tablet, twenty-three own both.* He draws a Venn diagram, and says, 'Find the probability that a pupil chosen at random owns a laptop, given that they own one device?' He writes twenty-three in the middle of the diagram where the two circles overlap. 'You have two minutes.'

I calculate the total number of classmates who own a laptop then divide that by the total number of classmates who own one device, which is fifty-one. I then divide twenty-nine by fifty-one. I input the numbers into my calculator. Venn diagrams are child's play. The teacher points at the boy on my right with his ruler, and says, 'The answer is?'

'Me nuh no,' mutters the boy.

'I don't know is what you mean.' The teachers here always correct boys when they speak creole. I raise my right arm. 'Yes Horatio?'

'Zero point five seven.'

'Correct.'

*

16:02 – School finished at three, and I am now at cricket practice at a training ground on the edge of St. John's, not far from the sea. Garfield is holding a cricket ball by its seam with his right thumb and index finger.

'Hold it like this.' He gives me the ball. 'And turn your hand out.' Garfield trots off and takes a batting position at the end of the cricket net. In the next net boys from my class are watching. I take a run up of three steps and bowl the ball. It spins through the air, Garfield swipes it with his bat, and calls out, 'You're a natural!' Some of the watching boys clap. I bowl some more balls, all of which are decent. Garfield trots over to me with his cricket bat clasped under his arm, bumps his fists against mine, and says, 'Talent.'

Cricket practice is over. I don't want to return to the house yet, so I go to the beach, paddle in the sea and look at the Venn diagrams in my maths textbook. *Easy.* I put the book in the mini rucksack on my back and continue paddling. This end of the beach is relatively quiet considering it is on the edge of St. John's. Most of the rest of it is taken up by a big resort. There are rows of sun loungers stretching nearly to the sea, and at the far end of the beach a marina with a cruise ship parked alongside.

On the beach close to where I am paddling are three tourists drinking bottled beer. Young adults – two women and a man. One of the women has long, silky blonde hair like Serena. Her face isn't half as nice as hers though. I am looking at the woman's hair when the man waves to me, and shouts, 'Hey bro?' *Looks like a dweeb.* 'What's up?'

'Not a lot. Been doing some Venn diagrams.'

'We can't hear you,' shouts the other woman, who has scruffy, brown hair. 'Come closer.' I go onto the beach. 'Are you from here, or are you a tourist?'

'I'm living here.'

The woman with the silky blonde hair prods the dweeb with her beer bottle. I hear her say, 'No way, too young.'

The woman with the scruffy brown hair says, 'What were you saying to us in the sea?' She looks at the dweeb. 'When he said, what's up?'

'Said I've been doing Venn diagrams.'

The dweeb says, 'Venn diagrams are those circles that cross over each other?'

'Yes.'

The dweeb says, 'Venn diagrams suck dude.'

No, you suck. He glugs beer. The brown-haired woman says, 'Why would you be doing Venn diagrams?' She sweeps the arm that is holding the beer bottle through the air. 'When you are in paradise.'

'Because I was learning about them at school today.'

The woman with the silky blonde hair says, 'Where are you from?'

'England.'

'We're Americans.'

I shrug my shoulders. The dweeb and the silky blonde-haired woman are whispering to each other. She raises her chin, and says, 'No way. Stupid idea.'

I say, 'What is a stupid idea?'

'Dude,' says the dweeb. 'We're looking for something.'

'Something, as in?'

Having looked over her shoulder, the woman with the brown hair says, 'Um, something illegal.'

I say, 'Drugs.'

The dweeb says, 'Know where we can get some?'

'If it's ganja you're after it's everywhere. I smell it all the time. Finding it will be as easy as finding baked beans in England. It's not even illegal.'

'Nah,' whispers the dweeb. 'We're after the white.'

They are all looking at me. I don't know where to get it… Actually, I do. There is the drug dealer with the bright blue mustang who lives in the shanty above the launderette. Could be money in this for me.

'I know someone.'

'Awesome!' blurts the dweeb.

'Can you hit us up?' says the woman with the brown hair.

'Maybe. I would have to go to his place as don't have his number on me.'

'Hold up,' says the dweeb. 'We're not giving you money up front.'

'Why not?'

He blows air from his mouth, and says, 'Forget it.'

Annoying that as only have ten EC on me. The dealer can keep my watch until I bring him the rest of the money. The brown-haired woman says, 'How's this going to play out then?'

'Give me your phone number. I'll phone if and when I get it. I'll bring it to you.'

'How long till you know?' says the dweeb.

'Depends on the bus. Between half an hour and forty minutes.'

'And the cost?' says the blonde.

'Will let you know when I phone.'

The dweeb says, 'We're in.'

I get their phone number and leave. On the bus, I look at the Venn diagrams in my textbook. If I had a smart phone, I'd find some more online. But I only have an outdated Nokia, Mum's father's old phone. If I can make some money selling drugs, I might buy a smart phone. Don't want to be seen by the manager or Dalilah if she happens to be about, so before getting off the bus I turn up my collar and put on my baseball cap. I get off at the bus stop and walk along the side of the road. The manager is on the launderette's porch chatting with a woman and not working as usual. I pull my baseball cap's bib forward, bow my head, and slink onto the track.

At the start of the shanty, the track forks left and right. I can see the dealer's bright blue mustang parked on the left, about sixty metres away. He must be in. Dalilah lives off the right side of the track, a minute's walk from here, in a tiny wooden house painted canary yellow. I saw it the Saturday before last when I went for a walk with her during my lunchbreak. Haven't been inside. Behind the dealer's car is a gate to a front yard. Inside the yard, a pit bull-type dog is prowling around. When it sees me, it rushes over to the gate, rears up on its hind legs and growls. Foam is spilling from its jaws. The door to the shack opens and the dealer comes out. Only ever seen him through the window of his car. He is quite tall, sort of sinewy, and has dirty looking braided dread-locks. The dog lowers its front paws to the ground and skulks off. As he strolls through the yard, the dealer hisses something in Creole. He's probably wondering what I'm doing here. I say, 'I'm after something.'

'Ganja?'

'Cocaine.' His eyes fix on me. They are red and squinted. He must recognise me, as he has seen me with Dalilah. 'How much?'

'Seventy.'

'A gramme?' He nods. 'Give me three.' The dealer rummages in the pocket of his shorts and takes out three tiny transparent seal bags with white powder in. Problem is I only have ten EC on me. He holds the bags up and clicks his fingers. 'Don't have money on me.' I take my watch off my wrist. *It's a Swatch worth one hundred and twenty pounds. Mum gave it to me for my birthday.* 'Keep this until I bring you the money tomorrow.'

The dealer shakes his head and says, 'Me nuh like dat.'

Nah like? He doesn't like my idea. 'Come on, why not? It's a Swatch worth four hundred EC.'

'Run weh.'

He turns around and walks off. I call after him, 'Come on, I'm telling the truth. You can find the watch on the internet. It's worth four hundred EC.'

He rotates his head and says, 'Wah mek yuh act so?'

He struts over to me, takes the watch, turns it over in his grubby fingers, then takes a phone from his shorts' pocket and searches for it on the internet. He pockets the watch and drops two of the tiny transparent seal bags into my palm.

'Said three.'

'Two.'

Ah! 'Will bring you the money at three forty-five tomorrow afternoon.'

'Alright.'

He grins. He has a gold-capped front tooth like Mum's ex-boyfriend Fool's Gold had. He walks off to the shack. The dog starts growling. When I turn around, I see someone leaning against the doorway of a shack on the other side of the track. It's that loser Javel. He is watching me. On the walk to the main road, I think about what to charge the tourists ... One hundred EC a gramme is

14

what I'm thinking. That is sixty EC in profit, which is approximately eighteen pounds. It would take over six hours to earn that in the launderette. This has only taken up an hour or so of my time, depending on how quickly the bus arrives that is. And it is a lot easier than heaving stinking laundry about in the searing heat.

*

An hour and a quarter later – Have just got back and am walking through the courtyard. Mum comes marching out of her father's house.

'Where have you been?'

'Was playing cricket. Told you that.'

'Don't walk away from me.' I stop walking. Mum plants her fists on her hips. 'Cricket practice only lasts an hour.'

'I went to the beach.'

'I need to know where you are and what you're doing. Sent you a text, you didn't reply. Why not?' I take out my phone. *So she did.* 'Well?'

'Didn't see it.'

'Okay. Don't do this again.'

Mum's stepmother is storming this way. She shouts, 'You can't just wander around, willy-nilly! You're still a kid.'

Bossy cow. I put the money in a sock in the chest of drawers in my bedroom, then switch on the aircon, lie on the bed, and use the iPad. Someone is knocking on the front door. I go downstairs and open it. It's Dougal.

'How tings?'

'Not too bad.'

He glances over his shoulder, waves a spliff in front of my nose, and says, 'Want some of dis?'

'Okay.'

As it's dark I put on mosquito repellent. Mum must be in the other house. Don't want her hearing me, so I walk through the

15

courtyard quietly, slip out of the gate, and go onto the waste ground beside the house. Frogs are croaking. Dougal sparks the spliff and takes several deep inhalations on it. Then he passes it to me. I suck on the spliff and cough. He chuckles.

'You're an amateur.'

'Don't smoke much.'

Tried cigarettes a couple of times but never smoked a spliff before. I take a weaker drag, hold the smoke in my lungs, and exhale. I take another drag and pass the spliff to him. Between drags he says, 'Remember dem crabs?'

'Yes.'

'Dis was de spot.'

'I know.'

'Dat was some dark shit, blowing dem up with firecrackers.' He passes me the spliff. 'Blamed me cos I'm older, but it wasn't my idea. Nightmare you caused me.'

'Are the crabs still here? Haven't seen any.'

'Some yeah. Most fled. News of dat slaying must've spread like wildfire.'

He passes me the spliff. I take a drag and pass it back to him. I feel relaxed and my senses are heightened. The frogs croaking is clearer than when I came out here. The spliff is finished. Dougal says he has somewhere to be and walks off. I squeeze through the courtyard gate. In the other house, I can hear Mum and her stepmother talking. However, I can't hear the words from here. I will tiptoe through the courtyard because it wouldn't be good if Mum heard me, as she would ask me where I've been. And she'll be suspicious if she finds out I was with Dougal. I am gently closing the gate when I hear the stepmother shriek, 'It's his father!'

Whose father? I tiptoe over to the house and press myself against the wall. A light is on in the living room, they must be in there. A mosquito screen has been pulled across the living room window, but the window is open. Can hear them quite clearly now. Mum says, 'Not ready to tell him yet.'

'Not ready? Or not willing?'

'Just not right now. Okay?'

'It is anything but okay. A boy cannot grow into a righteous and God-fearing man, if his life is built on a lie.'

'That's not fair Genevieve; I do my best by my son.'

It's my father they're talking about.

'How can it be the best, if it is a lie?'

'It's not a lie. It's just that one thing he doesn't know.'

'A big thing.'

'I will tell him, soon.' *Tell me what?* 'Have just had so much on my plate. My life was turned upside down by the death of my partner.' *Fool's Gold deserved everything he got.* 'Will tell him, I promise.'

'Get on with it. Your father is saying the same thing.'

'I know!'

What is Mum hiding? Behind me I hear the gate opening. I tiptoe quickly across the courtyard. It is Carlton and his daughter. He says, 'What's up?'

'Not a lot.'

Mum's stepmother comes out of the house, bends down, pats her knees, and says, 'Sweetie.'

The girl rushes into her arms. In my room, I pace in circles. Mum has been lying about my father all along. She is always brushing off questions I ask about him. What is she hiding from me? After banging my forehead on the wall several times, I get the mini cricket bat I brought with me from England from the chest of drawers. My father gave it to me when I was five, shortly before he disappeared forever. I sit on the side of the bed, hold the cricket bat by its handle and tap the base on the floor. If I ask Mum, she will know I was listening in. Which means if she doesn't tell me, and she probably won't, I can't ask her for ages. Ganja is supposed to be relaxing; but I'm feeling angry.

THREE

SUNDAY MORNING – Have just woken up. I roll over in bed and take my Swatch off the bedside table. I don't wear it in bed. It is 07:53. This morning the 'whole family' is going to a service at the cathedral. It will be boring. Antigua is supposed to be fun; a place people come to on holiday. If I was in London there would be no church, and I might be going to Serena's house. She would show off her new clothes; she always has new clothes. And I would watch her change into them. When I close my eyes, I see Serena bending over and pulling skimpy shorts over her slim, tanned legs. Her long, silky blonde hair is dangling nearly to the floor. I reach under the sheet and grip my cock.

'HORATIO!' *Ahh!* That's Mum calling from downstairs. 'Get up, get ready, and get over to the other house.'

'No! We're not leaving for church for ages. Want to stay in bed for a bit.'

'Just do it. I need to talk to you, it's important.'

Could be my father she wants to talk to me about. I leap out of bed, go to the bathroom, piss, brush my teeth, splash water on my face, pull on some clothes, and hurry over to the other house. Mum, her father and stepmother are huddled together on a sofa in the living room. The corners of their mouths are curled downwards. Do they know I've been smoking ganja with Dougal?

Mum says, 'Sit down please.' I sit on a chair. 'We have some

18

bad news, I'm afraid.' *What is it?* Mum looks at her father and then at me. 'It's Tanice.' *Aunt Fatso.* 'She's ill.' *And the bad news?* 'A-hhh.'

Her father puts his hand on her shoulder. Genevieve leans towards me, and says, 'Gravely ill. We must all pray for her in church today.'

I won't be. Mum lifts her head and says, 'It's cancer. The prognosis is bad; she may not even make it. She's had some tests done. We only just found out.' Mum weeps into her father's shoulder. *It's my father I want to hear about, not my aunt.* Mum grips onto my wrist and pulls me to her. *What are you hiding from me?* 'So sorry to start your day with such bad news.'

Her father wipes his eyes with his forearm, and says, 'Terrible news.'

I go to the other house, have some breakfast, then go upstairs, and get the two grammes of cocaine I scored off the dealer yesterday during my lunch break. They are for a tourist who phoned me when I was working in the launderette. He told me he got my number *off some yanks who'd stopped off on a ship for a couple of days.* I never gave them permission to give my number out. But it's money, easy money. He is in St. John's.

*

I am in the cathedral, sitting in the fourth pew from the front. Apart from Dougal they are all here. Mum is on my right, Genevieve is on my left. At the front of the cathedral, the priest is standing on a platform. He says, 'We will now sing hymn twenty-seven.'

Everyone stands up. I'm fed up with this endless singing. These Christian Antiguans are crazy about hymns. The service only started twenty minutes ago, and this is hymn number four.

'O God, our help in ages past,
our help for years to come,

our shelter from the stormy blast,
and our eternal ...'
Genevieve leans into me, and says, 'Sing louder, boy. We are
here to praise The Lord.'
I continue murmuring the words. Near the front of the cathedral, on either side of the aisle, are the choir. All women, all
wearing white. Many of them are old; nearly all of them are fat.
There are no Dalilah's here.
'Ha ha.'
Genevieve nudges me and says, 'Do not be laughing in the
house of The Lord.'
Mum pulls me to her and whispers, 'Don't be laughing for no
reason. Told you that plenty of times.'
'O God, our help in ages past,
our hope for years to come,
still be our guard while troubles last,
and our eternal home!'
I check the time on my Swatch. A girl goes to the front of the
cathedral and says, 'Proverbs Twelve, verses seventeen to twenty-
eight. Whoever speaks the truth gives honest evidence, but a false
witness utters deceit. There is one whose rash words are like sword
thrusts, but the tongue of the wise brings healing. Truthful lips
endure forever, but a lying tongue is but for a moment.' Mum
snorts. 'Deceit is in the heart of those who devise evil, but those who
plan peace have joy. No ill befalls the righteous, but the wicked are
filled with trouble. Lying lips are an abomination to the Lord ...'
Mum has squeezed her eyes shut. The priest says, 'We will now
sing hymn number forty-one.' Everyone stands up and starts
singing. I insert my hand into my trouser pocket and finger the
two bags of cocaine. When I arrived here, I asked the woman
handing out the order of service what time the service ended.
Then I texted my customer and told him to meet me outside in
the graveyard, ten minutes earlier than the service is meant to end
just in case it ends early. After the service the congregation will be

hanging around talking to each other. Will be easy to do the deal without being noticed. Everyone is getting on their knees. Genevieve whispers, 'Pray to The Lord that he will bring his healing power upon your aunt.'

No way! Genevieve is a bossy matriarch. Got that word, matriarch, in a spelling test at school this week. When I close my eyes, I see Aunt Fatso beached on a hospital bed, gorging on a giant packet of Maltesers.

'Ha ha ...'

I put my forearm over my mouth to stop myself laughing. The choir is singing another hymn. Jesus, these hymns are never ending. Everyone is moving into the central aisle to queue for communion. I stay put. Genevieve is coming back. *Ah!*

'What are you doing, boy? You can't receive communion as you're not confirmed. But you must receive a blessing for the sake of your soul.'

This woman is getting on my nerves bigtime. Mum told me I would have lots of fun in Antigua. She never mentioned churches or launderettes. Have just had a blessing from the priest and am heading to my pew when my phone *beeps*. It's a text.

....

Today, Now

Where r u?

....

The moment the service ends, I go outside. Everyone is talking to each other and they won't notice I'm not there. In the graveyard, there is a scrawny, shifty-looking white man. He is watching me. People are spilling out of the cathedral. Best get this deal done. I walk past him with my head turned away from him.

21

'Put the money on the grave on your right. Don't look at me.'

He does it. I grab the money, and with my back to the cathedral count it. He steps towards me.

'Give me the gear.'

'Stay there and don't look at me.'

I put the two bags of cocaine on the grave on my left. He picks them up.

'HORATIO!'

Genevieve, damn! The man is skulking off. They are in a group by the entrance to the cathedral, watching me. Mum has her fists on her hips. She says, 'What were you doing over there with that strange man?'

'I was checking out the graveyard. That man started talking to me.'

Genevieve says, 'That man is no servant of Christ. He has no place here, in the house of The Lord.'

*

07:50 – The following Saturday – Can hear Mum downstairs talking to someone on the phone. She is coming upstairs.

'Horatio!'

'What?'

'Don't what me. You mean, good morning Mum.'

'Good morning, Mum.'

'Your sister is on the phone. Can I come in?' She comes in even though I haven't said it's okay for her to. 'When you're done bring the phone downstairs.'

I take the phone off her, and say into it, 'Hello.'

'Horatio, hey. How's everything going over there?'

'Fine.'

'Um, well I'm not fine. Finding it hard to sleep and it's difficult to concentrate at college. So worried about our aunty. You know the diagnosis is bad?'

'I know.'

'She might die. Ah, she'll probably die.'

'Oh.'

'Is that all you have to say?'

I don't say anything. My sister says, 'Mum is having a hard time. She was trying to put on a brave face for me, but I can tell she is suffering inside. They are so close. Must be hard being there when her sister is so ill … Mum needs your support right now. Do you understand?'

'Yes.'

My sister says by support, she means being understanding and caring, and doing my best to make her life easier at this difficult time. Again, she asks me if I understand. Again, I say 'Yes.'

'Okay, speak soon. *Bye.*'

What about me? Mum hasn't told me what she knows about my father; what she's been hiding from me for ages.

*

I haul a bundle of bedding from the washing machine, lug it over to a drying machine, and stuff it inside. After wiping my damp forearms with a hand towel, I look at my maths textbook. On the page there is a tree diagram with a description above it. *The probability that a boxer wins the first round of a fight is 3/5. If he wins the first round, the probability that he wins the second round is 9/10. If he loses the first round, the probability—*

'Take your break now.' The manager has waddled out of the office. 'Big delivery coming at one.'

I take the textbook, fill a plastic cup with water from the filter machine, and go onto the porch. Haven't been there long when I see Javel loping this way. He stops in front of the launderette.

'Wah gwaan white bwoy?'

I hold the maths textbook up, and say, 'Studying conditional probability.'

He sticks his right middle finger up at me and laughs – 'Hah hah.'

Ah! 'Have a conditional probability question for you here.' I pretend I'm reading from the maths textbook. 'If you were born a loser, and have always been a loser, what is the probability of you growing up to be a loser …?' He snarls and sticks his middle finger up at me again. 'Well?'

'Chupitness.'

'Wrong answer. The answer is it's a certainty.'

He spits on the ground, approaches the steps leading up to the porch, mumbles something in Creole, and says, 'Fuck you!'

He steps onto the bottom step. The manager comes onto the porch and shouts, 'Away with you! You're not welcome here.'

'Highty tiety ooman.' He aims his right and middle index fingers at me. 'Bang! Bang!'

'Away with you!'

'Scunt!'

He lopes off to the track. The manager sighs and says, 'Bad minded dunce that boy.' She is pointing at me. 'Stay away from the ragamuffin, he's bad news. He is jealous of you because Dalilah likes you. She don't like him. What girl would? He looks like a rat; he'd give a girl nightmares.'

'Chupitness, he said. What does that mean?'

'Talking nonsense.'

'I wasn't. And he said to you highty tiety. What's that?'

'A conceited person who looks down at others.'

'And scunt?'

'Take the S off the front, same meaning.' She shakes her head. 'Terrible.'

My phone *beeps*. It is a text from that druggie from the grave-yard. He wants rock this time, two hundred EC's worth. By rock he means crack. I've heard the term before on TV. The dealer will have crack. I text the druggie I won't be available until Monday. He texts almost immediately asking if I can do today. I text back saying no. He texts – *Okay, I'm in.* Will meet him during school lunchbreak in the graveyard again. I will buy the drugs after my shift. Always keeping money on me now just in case a tourist is after any. A van has pulled up in front of the launderette. It will be dirty bed linen from a resort near here. I take the bags out of the van and the van drives off. Dalilah is skipping towards me. She is with another teenage girl. Dalilah shrieks 'Hi' and throws her arms around my neck.

The other girl says, 'Pretty handsome.'

'You bet,' says Dalilah.

'Clever too I hear. How's island life treating you?'

'Other than the launderette, it's alright.'

The girl says, 'People are nice, right?'

'Most of them are okay. Well, not that loser, Javel.'

Dalilah says, 'Pankoot.'

'Pankoot?'

'Pankoot,' says Dalilah, 'is an idiot.'

The other girl says, 'You'll pick up the creole.'

The manager calls out from the porch, 'Good afternoon, girls.'

'Good afternoon.'

'Horatio,' says the manager. 'Get them bags up here.'

Ah, bossy she is. Dalilah kisses me on the cheek, and says, 'We'll leave you to it.'

The shift has just ended, and I am walking up the track to the shanty. It's sticky. I push down the top of the mini rucksack on my back and press the cold can of Coca-Cola I'm holding to the side of my neck. I text the dealer. He gave me his number. When I get close to the dealer's property, the dog in the yard growls. The dealer comes out of the shack, walks over to the gate, drapes his arm over it, bumps his fist against mine, and says, 'Wah gwaan, yute?'

'I'm after one hundred and forty EC's worth of crack.'

'Alright.'

When he goes inside the shack, the dog starts growling again. I have this feeling that someone is watching me. When I turn around, I see Javel slouched on the porch of the shack on the other side of the track. He goes inside the shack. The dealer comes out, passes me the drugs, and says, 'Gimme it.'

I give him the money, put the drugs in the pocket of my shorts, and head back the way I came. At the bus stop, I sit on its bench and sip Coca-Cola … Fifteen minutes have passed, and the bus still hasn't arrived. It's nearly dark. I am looking up the long stretch of road in the direction that the bus will be coming in. There are some cars and a van, but no bus. I can see flashing blue lights. Police, must be. Could they be coming for me? It is very unlikely, but just in case, I take the plastic film-wrapped drugs from my pocket, reach down and stuff them through the opening in the now empty Coca-Cola can, which is on the ground by my feet. With my heel I nudge the can away from me. A police pickup truck screeches to a halt in front of the bus stop, and a policeman in a light blue shirt and navy-blue baseball cap jumps out and rushes over to me. I start standing up.

'Stay seated.' I lower myself down. 'What're you doing here?'

'Waiting for a bus.'

A policewoman exits the pickup truck and comes over. The policeman says, 'Stand up, turn around.' I do it. With his foot he pushes my feet apart. The policeman pats me down from my ankles up to my collar. Meanwhile, the policewoman rummages in my mini rucksack. She stops rummaging, zips it up, and places it on the ground beside me. The policeman tells me to turn around, which I do. He has a wide face and sunken eyes.

'What're you doing here?'

'Waiting for a bus. Told you already.'

'You're not from here.' He grips onto the sides of his belt. 'You a tourist?'

'I'm English, but I'm living here now.'

'Where do you stay?'

'Twenty minutes up the road near Saint Martin.'

'What are you doing here?'

26

'Been working at the launderette across the road. It belongs to my mother's father.'

'Bevis Robinson.'

'Yes.'

The policeman steps back and says, 'That'll be all.'

They get into the pickup truck and drive off. They were looking for drugs. This means someone must have tipped them off. Other than the dealer, the only person who likely knew I just scored was that loser, Javel.

*

Monday lunchtime – I am in the graveyard. Here comes the druggie. He looks like shit – dirty, black bags under his eyes, and doesn't smell great either. He says 'Hi,' and takes a one hundred EC note from the pocket of his tattered shorts. 'Thing is, um, just got a hundred on me now. Waiting on a bank transfer. Should have come in this morning.' *Ahh!* 'Will definitely get the money tomorrow at the latest. Is it alright if I give you the other hundred then?'

'No.'

'Come on man, give me a break, trying my best here.'

'One hundred gets you half of it.'

I take the banknote off him and unwrap the plastic film covering the drugs. There are four rocks of crack inside. I place two rocks in his palm.

'Come on man give me the rest on tick, will have the money tomorrow.' I wrap the remaining rocks up in the plastic film. 'Don't make me score off the street. Will get ripped off.'

I walk away from the dirty druggie. In future I want to sell to rich tourists, not scum like him. Will ignore him if he contacts me again. This is annoying, what am I going to do with the rest of it? Will have to wait until I find someone looking for crack. Until then will keep it in my sock drawer.

The first class of the afternoon is English. The teacher is discussing *Of Mice and Men*. The class read it last term. *Of Mice and Men* is a novella written by John Steinbeck. I read it a few weeks back. Only took me three hours or so to read. It is about two migrant ranch workers in California during the Great Depression. The teacher is asking questions.

'Garfield.'

'Yes, Sir.'

'The book has various themes. Name one?'

'Dreams.'

'Yes.'

'Ezequiel, give me another?'

'Loneliness.'

'Horatio. *Of Mice and Men* is taught in many schools all over the world. However, it has also been targeted by censors. Why would that be?'

'Because of what the censors perceive to be the book's offensive and racist language.'

'Precisely. *Of Mice and Men* is on the American Library Association's list of the Most Challenged Books of the Twenty-First Century.'

I know, read all about it on the iPad at the house.

FOUR

THURSDAY – IT IS LATE AFTERNOON, and I have just got back to the house. Mum is sitting at the table in the living room area, fiddling with a bunch of keys.

'There you are. Had a good day?'

'It was fine.'

'Nothing to report then?'

'No.'

'I need to talk to you about something.'

'Sure.'

Does she want to talk about her ill sister again, or is she finally going to tell me what she's been hiding about my father. Mum is nibbling on her left little finger's nail. She stands up and says, 'Would you like some iced tea?'

'Yes, please.'

Mum takes a bottle of iced tea from the fridge and pours it into two glasses. When she carries the glasses over to the table, several drops splash on the floor. I have a gulp of iced tea. She interlocks the fingers of both hands together and looks up at the ceiling. She separates her hands, pulls her chair closer to mine, and says, 'Want to talk to you about your father.'

Finally! 'Go ahead. What?'

'I haven't told you everything.' *Know that.* She sighs. 'You have to understand I did it to protect you.' Mum strokes my knee. 'You were just too young to know the details. That's why I've waited until now to tell you.'

'Tell me what?'

'*Ah*, I told you he disappeared.'

'Yes, when I was five.'

'Must have been tough on you.' Mum interlocks her fingers again. 'Really tough.'

'Mum, tell me!'

'Er, disappeared wasn't exactly what happened to him.'

'Speak up, you're murmuring.'

Mum leans back in the chair, lowers her head, and says, 'Your father didn't disappear.'

'What happened to him then? Tell me!'

'H-he died.'

'Died! How do you know?'

'Because I know.'

'How? If he disappeared, you wouldn't know.'

She puts her elbows on the table, and says, 'Th-the police told me, that's how.'

'The police told you my father is dead?'

'Yes.'

'When did this happen?' She opens and closes her mouth. 'When, I said? I need to know.' She opens her mouth again, then closes it without having said anything. 'MUM!'

She looks up at the ceiling and says in a quiet voice, 'When you were five.'

'Five!' I bang my fist on the table. 'I'm fifteen. That was a decade ago.'

'You were too young to know.'

'Rubbish!' I jump to my feet. 'How was I too young when I was nine, ten eleven to know the truth?'

'A-hh, sit down please.' I punch my palm and drop onto the chair. 'W-was trying to do my best by you.' *Sniff.* 'Perhaps I shouldn't have waited so long.'

'Of course you shouldn't!'

'A-hh, know that.' She runs the fingers of her right hand through her tied back curly brown hair. 'I'm so sorry.'

She touches my knee. I pull my leg away, and say, 'How did he die?' Mum blows air from her mouth. I stand up. 'Tell me, now!'

'Sit down and I will tell you.' I drop onto the chair. 'H-he was, *hhh*, er—'

'Tell me, I said!'

'H-he was killed.'

'Killed?'

'Yes, your father was shot.'

'Shot! Who shot him?'

'A-hh, don't know the exact details, only what I was told. Didn't want to know any more, just wanted it all to go away. It was so difficult to deal with. And I was on my own, and—'

'Who shot him?' She has covered her face with her hands. She removes them and shoves them in her lap. 'Mum!'

'It happened in London. Another man was, *hh*, shot as well. Police said they shot each other.'

'Oh my God! Can't believe you've waited until now to tell me this.' I bang both fists on the table. 'What happened?'

'Don't know all the details.' *Sniff.* She wipes her eyes with her sleeve. 'Seems your father was involved in something he shouldn't have been. No idea what it was.'

'What else aren't you telling me?'

Mum looks at me and says, 'Nothing. Told you everything I know. Have a death certificate and letters from the police in London. When we're back there, you can see everything. Okay?'

'Okay! You've lied to me for a decade. It's anything but okay.'

'Didn't mean to hurt you.' She grabs my arm; I pull it away. 'It was to protect you.'

'Liar.'

'Didn't want you to carry that burden around with you,' *sniff*, 'when you were young. I understand you are upset, but you have

31

to understand I did this for you.' *Want to be on my own.* I get up, stomp upstairs, go into my room, slam the door shut, and fall face first onto the bed. Mum is knocking on the door. 'Horatio!'

'Leave me alone.'

'Just because your father was involved in crime, it doesn't mean you will turn out that way.'

I hear her walk off. How dare that lying bitch pretend my father had disappeared when she knew all along he was dead. So, this is what she has been hiding. If her stepmother hadn't told her to tell me the truth, she might never have told me. I thump the pillow. Does everyone else know? Was I the last person to find out? I chuck the pillow across the room. When I return to London, want to see the death certificate and those letters from the police. I get off the bed and pace in circles around the room. What was my father involved in that led to him being shot? I stop pacing and sit on the bed. Been in this position for about forty minutes when I hear footsteps on the stairs, and now knocking on my door.

'Yes.'

'Horatio.'

'What, Mum?'

'Can I come in?'

'No.'

'We're making pasta soon. Come join us in the other house and have some. Horatio ... *Horatio.*'

'Yes.'

'Did you hear what I just said?'

'Yes.'

'Will you come over and join us?'

'No.'

'Don't want you being on your own all evening.' I don't say anything. 'A-hh, will bring dinner over when it's ready. We can have it together here.'

*

The next day – I'm in English. We have just started *Jane Eyre* by Charlotte Brontë. It is one of the texts from the syllabus. I have read *Wuthering Heights*, which was written by Charlotte's sister Emily. *Wuthering Heights* is quite tedious and turgid. Turgid means bloated and longer than it needs to be. *Jane Eyre* is going to be the same. How dare Mum not tell me the truth about my father. I scrunch up a piece of paper underneath the desk. The teacher says, 'Ezequiel, you are going to start us off.'

Ezequiel stands up and opens his copy of *Jane Eyre* – 'There was no possibility of taking a walk that day. We had been wandering, indeed, in the leafless shrubbery an hour in the morning; but since dinner (Mrs Reed, when there was no company, dined early) the cold winter wind had brought with it clouds so sombre, and a rain so penetrating, that further out-door exercise was now out of the question. I was glad of it: I never liked long walks, especially on chilly afternoons: dreadful to me was the coming home in the raw twilight, with nipped fingers and toes, and a heart saddened by the chidings of …'

Last night I tried to find out more about what happened to my father on the internet. Found a couple of short newspaper articles. The police discovered three bodies in a block of flats in London. My father Dyson Devereux, a Moldovan called Maria Cebotari, and an Albanian national name unknown. An article from a borough newspaper had quotes from the police, saying my father and the Albanian shot each other, and that the Moldovan woman was shot by the Albanian. But why? What was he doing in that flat in the first place? None of it makes sense. *Ahh!* I grab a pencil off the desk and snap it in half.

'Horatio!' says the teacher. 'Why did you snap that pencil?' I shrug my shoulders and don't say anything. 'Stand up and read.'

I pick up my copy of *Jane Eyre* and stand up. Where have they got to? Here's the place – 'Folds of scarlet drapery shut in my view

33

to the right hand; to the left were the clear panes of glass, protecting, but not separating me from the drear November day. At intervals, while turning over the leaves of my book, I studied the aspect of that winter afternoon. Afar, it offered a pale blank of mist and cloud; near a scene of wet lawn and storm-beat shrub, with ceaseless rain sweeping away wildly before a long and lamentable blast.'

'That will do.' I sit down. *Beep.* That was my phone. I take it out of my trouser pocket. It is a text from Mum asking if I'm alright. No, I'm not, thanks to you. I always take the bus to school, but this morning her father drove me. In the car, he talked about my school and cricket. He didn't mention my father. 'Garfield.'

'I cannot tell what sentiment haunted the quite solitary churchyard, with its inscribed headstone; its gate, its two trees, its low horizon, girdled by a broken wall, and its newly-risen crescent, attesting the hour of eventide ...'

*

19:01 – I am in my room doing algebra homework. It is pretty easy; maths always is. Finding it hard to concentrate though. When I got back here from school, I searched the internet for more about my father. Found some stuff about the work he did at borough councils. He was the boss of the Burials and Cemeteries department at a couple of councils. Didn't find anything more about his death though. I lie on the bed, put my hands behind my head, and look up at the rotating fan hanging from the ceiling. Where is he buried? Did he leave me anything?

'Horatio, I'm *home.*' Mum was here when I arrived. She has just been to the shops. I can hear her coming up the stairs. There is a knock on my door. 'Can I come in?'

'Yes.'

She enters the room, sits on the end of my bed, taps me on the lower leg, and says, 'Got the stuff we needed from the shops ...

34

Everyone is so friendly and welcoming over here. Makes a big change from London, that's for sure.' She taps my leg again. 'How was your day? I didn't get much of a chance to speak to you when you got in from school.'

'Not too bad.'

'What were you learning about at school today? Anything new?'

'We started reading *Jane Eyre*.'

'Ah, who wrote that again? Was it Dickens?'

'Was Brontë, Charlotte Brontë.'

'Of course it was.' Again, she taps my leg. 'What else did you do at school?'

'What is this, forty questions?'

'Asking because I care. That's what mothers do.'

'Where is my father buried?' Mum looks up at the ceiling and blows air from her nose. 'Mum!'

'Your father was cremated. His ashes are in a cemetery in the countryside, where his family are from. Can't remember where exactly.' She taps her chin. 'Devon, I think, or it might be Dorset. Have a letter at home in London with the details. Can dig it out when we're there.' She strokes my leg. 'Okay?'

'Did he leave me anything?'

Mum *huffs* and says, 'Yeah, there are a few things. I will give them to you when we return to London.'

'What else do you know about him being shot?'

She *huffs* and says, 'Nothing.'

'Nothing! You must know about the others shot in that flat. The Albanian and—'

'I told you someone else was shot, that the police said they shot each other. Please just leave it. This isn't helping.'

'Never said anything though did you about the Moldovan woman, Maria Cebotari.'

'Enough!' Mum stands up. 'Did what I thought was right. Now I'm sorry I didn't tell you earlier. But I did it for you.' She is

35

pointing at me. 'Appreciate it's difficult for you, I really do. But looking up stuff on the internet won't help … And what about me? You have no idea how difficult it's been bringing you up all on my own. And now look what I'm going through with my sister.' *Sniff.* 'Not once have you asked how she is, or how I'm coping. Everyone else has. Your sister, and everyone here.'

'Where did you two meet?'

'A-hh, at Newton Borough Council. We were both working there.'

That makes sense. She leaves the room and closes the door behind her. I remain on the bed peering up at the whirling fan. Haven't been doing it for long when there is a knock on the door.

'Yeah.'

'Horatio.'

'What?'

'Come over to the other house in twenty minutes. We're going to have dinner there. Something special … Horatio!'

'Yes.'

'Did you hear what I said?'

'Yeah.'

Can hear her walking downstairs, and now the front door closing. I go downstairs and check the fridge. There is only salad and eggs. Looks like I'll be going to the other house.

*

Twenty minutes later – Mum, her father and Genevieve are at the dining table. When I walk in her father gets up, slaps me on the shoulder, and says, 'Horatio, right on time as always. Take a pew.'

There is a place set between Mum and Genevieve. I would prefer to take my food and eat in the other house. But they'd just say no, so I sit down. Mum places her hand on my knee, and asks, 'How are you feeling?'

'Hungry.'

Her father says, 'That's what we like to hear.'

Genevieve picks up pieces of fried chicken with tongs and puts them on my plate. Then she puts some rice and salad on my plate. I say, 'Thank you.'

'You're welcome.'

The chicken tastes better than KFC, better than any fried chicken I've ever had. The adults are chatting to each other. My father would have known who wrote *Jane Eyre*. Mum leans into me and whispers, 'Is everything okay?'

'Yeah.'

Her father says, 'Horatio was telling me this morning in the car about his bowling. Got three wickets in the nets at practice last week. All spin bowls.'

'Darling,' says Mum, 'you never told me about your bowling skills.'

I swallow my mouthful of food, and say, 'Only just started bowling, but I'm already good at it. Spin bowling comes naturally to me.'

'Modesty is a virtue,' says Genevieve.

'Next month,' says Mum's father, 'New Zealand are touring the West Indies. One of the tests is being played here. We will go.'

I put a piece of chicken in my mouth. Genevieve says, 'Say thank you.'

I swallow the chicken, and say, 'Great.'

'Will be fun,' says Mum. 'It'll be your first cricket match.'

The adults are talking to each other. My father must've liked cricket because he bought me a mini cricket bat when I was five. If he was still alive, I would already have been to a cricket match. *Beep.* I take my phone out of my pocket. Genevieve says, 'No phones at the table.'

It is a text from Dougal, asking if I want to come over … Dinner is finished. Genevieve tells me to help clear up. While rinsing plates under the tap in the sink, I say to Mum, 'Dougal's invited me over to his.'

37

'Oh, okay.' I put the plates in the dishrack. Mum is looking at me. Her eyes have sort of narrowed. 'What are you planning to do over there?'

'Watch TV, play games, I guess.'

'And you want to go?'

'Yeah, might as well.'

Her father is whispering to her. Think he said *Will do him some good.* Mum says, 'Fine. But don't be any later than ten-thirty. And don't be heading off anywhere else without speaking to me first. And if I phone, answer.'

'Fine.'

'Have fun,' she says. 'And be good.'

Her father follows me out of the house. In the courtyard he says, 'Things might not be easy for you at the moment. But bear in mind they are not easy for your mother either. This is a difficult time with Tanice being so ill.' He taps me on the shoulder. 'Have fun.'

Dougal lives about three minutes' walk from here in a tiny wooden house on the main road. It is painted bright blue and has a lawn with a fence around it. Dougal is on a chair on the porch.

'Wa gwaan, Cuz?'

'Not a lot. Was just eating fried chicken.'

'Genevieve's fried chicken is de best.' He stands up. 'Come on in.' Inside, there is a tiny living room with some chairs, a table, a television, and along the far wall a fridge, stove, and a counter with some crockery on it. 'Want a cold one?'

'Cold one?'

'Beer.'

'Sure.'

Dougal takes two bottles of beer from the fridge, removes the caps, and passes one to me. The beer is called Carib. It is a popular brand on the island. He clinks his bottle against mine, and says, 'Cheers.' I have a gulp of beer. 'Toiled in dat launderette for a whole summer. Hot as hell 'n seething with mosquitos.'

'What are you doing now?'

'Road maintenance.' He has a swig of beer. 'Like de camaraderie 'n de banter. On your own in de launderette, other than de manager. Nice lady, Hyacinth. Bossy mind.' He holds his beer bottle out towards me. 'Seen de girl who lives up the hill from de launderette? Caramel skin, brown curly hair. Teenage beauty queen.'

'Dalilah.'

He clicks his fingers, and says, 'Yeah, dat's her name. You met her?'

'Yes, we hang out all the time.'

'You're playing with me.'

'I'm telling the truth.'

Dougal blows air from his mouth, and says, 'You're fantasising, Cuz?'

I find Dalilah's number on my phone. *Beeep… Beeep… Beeep … Beee—*

'Hey honey, what's up?' I press the hands-free button. 'At my auntie's. Can't talk for long.'

'Dalilah, I'm at my cousin's house having a beer.'

'Nice.'

'He was just talking about you.' Dougal presses the base of his palms to his forehead. 'He worked at the launderette last summer.'

'Yeah, remember that boy. Stumpy dreads, few years older than you.'

'That's him. Goodbye.'

'Bye.'

I hang up. Dougal says, 'Shit.' He inflates and deflates his cheeks, then gets a bag of ganja, some rolling papers and a pouch of tobacco from a drawer. 'Don't you be telling your mother you've been smoking with me. I don't want to be taking de blame. Got it?'

'Yes.'

39

I lean forward in my chair and watch him prepare a spliff. I could do that. He says, 'Smoke it outside.' We go onto the porch. He sparks the spliff. On the path leading to the house there is a land crab. It scuttles off into the grass. 'Must've seen you, cos dat crab was in a big hurry.' He exhales smoke from his mouth, then passes me the spliff. I have a couple of drags on it and pass it back to him. After smoking it we go inside. He picks up a framed photograph of a smiling black woman off the table in the living room. 'Gone six years my mother, God bless her soul. Brain tumour. Saw her when you visited when you were little. Remember?'

'No.'

'She remembered you alright.' He has a glug of beer. 'How's de old man faring?'

'The old man?'

'Your grandfather, my great uncle. Who else? Terrible news about Tanice. De cancer is bad is what I hear. Feel for what he's going through, really do. Worst time of my life it was my mother being sick. Awful. Wouldn't want anyone to experience dat misery, let alone my own flesh 'n blood … Salt of de earth he is. Been a father 'n grandfather to me what with my father being overseas 'n my grandfather, your great uncle, deceased.'

Dougal is flicking through the television channels. Why was my father in that flat with those two foreigners? Why did they shoot each other? And why did Mum not tell me till now?

'Premier League,' he says. 'You watch it?'

There is football on. I say, 'No, don't watch football.'

'World Cup, dat's it for me. I'm into cricket 'n basketball.' He continues flicking through the channels. He stops on a music channel. 'Listen to dat beat.'

He is tapping his fingers on the arm of his chair in time with the reggae music. I say, 'It's okay.'

'Okay?' He tilts towards me. 'Embrace the Caribbean vibe, Cuz.' Dougal is prodding at the television. 'Check out de jiving girl with platted hair on de right. *Fine!* Her face is nice, but she has a huge round arse. 'A twenty-something Dalilah.'

'A Dalilah who lives on a diet of McDonalds.'

Beer spurts from Dougal's mouth onto the floor – 'Hah! *Funny.*' He stops flicking through the channels and starts making another spliff. I think about my father. 'Your poor mother's been through hell. Moves here 'n her sister falls ill straight away.' He stops flicking through the channels. 'Tell me if I'm out of order asking dis. Her partner died right? Not long before you guys came here.' *Fool's Gold.* 'How'd he go? Disease?'

'Erotic asphyxiation gone wrong.'

'Come again?'

'Erotic asphyxiation gone wrong. Accidentally strangled himself to death while getting off.'

'Getting off?'

'He used to wank, jerk off, while strangling himself.' Dougal lifts his eyebrows. 'This fetish is called erotic asphyxiation, EA for short.' Dougal's mouth is hanging open. 'It's true, my mum's boyfriend was into erotic asphyxiation.'

'Hold up!' Dougal raises his hands. 'Never heard of dis twisted EA shit. Either I'm naïve, or it's bullshit.'

'You're naive. Loads of weirdos get off having their air cut off.'

'Not in Antigua and Barbuda dey don't. Never heard nothing of it, anyhow.'

'That's because erotic asphyxiation is a taboo.'

'No shit!' He licks the cigarette paper and rolls a perfect, conical-shaped spliff. Watched him make one twice now and I know exactly how to do it. He waves the spliff in the air. 'Have dis after we finish dis conversation. Don't want de neighbours hearing it.' He *snorts.* 'Mean to tell me dat while you're getting it on with your Dalilah, and me with my McDonald's Dalilah, some dude is making do with a noose.'

'Yes.'

'Sweet Jesus!'

41

'That is what my mum's idiot boyfriend was doing when he died. We saw him in the living room dead with a noose around his neck and pornography playing on—'

'Enough!' Dougal holds his right palm out at me. 'Don't believe any of dis. Regardless, it's disrespect. It's your mother you're talking about. Well, her partner.'

'It's true, I swear. The coroner's verdict was—'

'Enough I said.' He stands up. 'Coming?'

We go onto the porch and he lights the spliff. A mosquito lands on my forearm. I squash it with my hand. Between drags, Dougal mutters something that sounds like *Shit*. He passes me the spliff. After smoking it we go inside. My head is feeling heavy. Colours are swirling on the wall.

'You alright?'

'A bit stoned.'

'Not used to it. Takes practice.' He points at me. 'Don't be mixing too much drink with de ganja, if you're not used to it. Dis will be your last.' He passes me a bottle of beer. 'I'm on de rum.'

Dougal pours rum into a glass then flicks through the television channels. Why did my father die? If he had a gun with him, he must've known something was about to happen? Why did he have a gun in the first place …? Was he a secret agent? Dougal is watching basketball. How dare Mum not tell me till now! What was she thinking?

'You looked stressed, paranoid.'

'I'm fine.'

'Alright … BOOM!' Dougal jumps off his chair. 'Check de replay, Cuz. Unreal!' A player dribbles the ball up to an opposing player, spins three hundred and sixty degrees, dribbles down the court, leaps through the air and does a slam dunk. I have a gulp of beer. 'De Raptors 'n de Nets are going at it.' *Should have been told what happened to him ages ago.* He jumps off the chair again and waves his right middle and index fingers in the air. 'Three points!' He falls back onto the chair. 'All square.'

42

Basketball is boring. What happened in that flat? Why did my father die? I want to know.

'Ah!'

'Say something?'

'No.'

'Cuz, what're you rubbing your head for? Watch de game.'

Dougal has a swig of rum. My father was in charge of a department at a borough council, so why would he have a gun? Was he a gangster? None of it makes sense. I'm feeling stressed out. So much for ganja being relaxing … Wonder what crack feels like? People say it makes them feel good … That crack is still in my sock drawer.

'Where you going?'

'Out. Will be back in a few minutes.'

'Alright. REBOUND! End to end dis.' He calls after me, 'Don't let your mother see you. Eyes are bloodred. Tell-tale.'

In the courtyard, I hear Bossy talking loudly in the other house. The lights and fans are off. Mum must be in the other house, or somewhere else. In my bedroom, I open the chest of drawers and take from the sock the plastic film-wrapped rocks of crack. I put on some mosquito repellent and return to Dougal's. When I go inside, he is swigging rum.

'Drunk.' He plunks the glass on the table. 'Game's done. Raptors messed it up.' I put the crack on the table next to his glass. 'What's dat?'

'Crack.'

'Tap lie!'

'Tap lie?'

'Stop lying.' Dougal picks up the crack and holds it up to his eyes. He is shaking his head from side to side, which makes his stumpy dreadlocks flap about. 'Where'd you get dis?'

'From a dealer.'

'Just now?'

'No, a while ago. Was for someone else.'

43

'You smoked dis shit before?'

'No, never.'

'Our family find out about dis, you're in big shit. Know dat right? Talking crabs times ten.'

'Yes. Just want to try it once, to see what it's like.'

'It's addictive, bigtime. You seen de junkies in Saint Jan's living on de street, smelling high, flies on dem. You think any of dem when they smoked it de first time said, I'll smoke it till I'm eating out of dumpsters. Do you?'

'You ever smoked it?'

'Hell no! Snorted some lines of powder at a couple of parties, dat's it.'

'Want to know what it's like, don't you?'

His mouth is twitching. He pours some rum into his glass, downs it, wipes his lips, and says, 'Don't be bringing me into dis.'

Crack can be smoked off tinfoil. I say, 'Do you have tinfoil?'

He shrugs his shoulders. In a cupboard next to the stove, I find a roll of kitchen foil. I tear off two strips. Dougal is gripping onto dreadlocks on the sides of his head. He doesn't like smoking inside, so I take his lighter off the table, a strip of tinfoil and the crack, and head for the door.

'Don't you be smoking off tinfoil on my porch!' I sit down. 'Dragging me into de depths of hell, Cuz. Déjà vu.' I unwrap the crack, take out a rock and rotate it in my fingertips. It is quite big. 'Don't be smoking all dat!'

'Why not?'

'Look at the size of it, you'll have a heart attack. Halve it.'

He gets a knife, takes the rock off me, and cuts it in half. Need to suck the smoke up with something. On a shelf there is a pad of paper. I tear off a piece, rip it in half, and roll one of the halves into a cone shape. Dougal downs his glass of rum, then turns around the photograph of his dead mother, so that it is facing the wall. With my thumb I make a depression in a strip of tinfoil. I drop the half rock into it, put one end of the rolled-up piece of paper in my mouth, grip the rim of the tinfoil, and light it from underneath. The smoke tastes bitter. I have a major headrush. I drop the lighter and the tinfoil, and spit the paper from my mouth. My heartbeat is pounding in my ears.

'What's it like …? Cuz!'

'Powerful!' I jump up from the chair and punch the air. Feel strong, feel energised. 'RAHHH!'

I drop onto the chair. Can clearly hear the tree frogs croaking outside. My whole body is shuddering. I close my eyes and grip onto the sides of the chair. Waves of power are surging through me. I open my eyes. Little cracks and pieces of frayed paint have appeared on the walls. Before they were just bare white walls. My head feels huge. I can't feel any other part of my body. It's like my body and limbs have disappeared and I am now all head. A head full of power; a god head … Dougal is holding a piece of tinfoil and he has a rolled-up piece of paper in his mouth.

Can barely hear the tree frogs croaking now and the walls are bare white again. Dougal is staring up at the ceiling. His chest is heaving in and out.

'Extreme,' he says. 'All-consuming.' Dougal is squinting at me. 'Secret dis, between you 'n me. Others get wind of it, we'll be pariahs. I'll get most of de blame like last time cos I'm older. Can't be dealing with dat. Get me?'

'Yeah.'

'Hard drugs been tearing our community apart. Dey're enemy number one. 'N don't be saying nothing to Dalilah, dat girl won't tolerate crack. Another thing. Don't be poling up here with crack again. Done with it. It's eternal damnation.'

My phone is ringing. It's Mum. I answer – 'Hello.'

'How're you two getting on over there?'

Dougal smacks his forehead with the base of his palm. I say, 'Fine, Mum.'

'What're up to?'

'Just watched some basketball. Raptors versus Nets.'

45

'Okay. Well come back soon.'

'I will.'

'Good boy. Bye.'

Dougal is biting on a fingernail and eyeing the remaining crack rock on the table. It's time to go. I pick up the crack and leave ... I enter the house and gently push the front door closed. On the stairs, I hear music coming from Mum's room. She is probably using the iPad. When I step onto the landing, she says, 'Did you have fun?'

'Yes.'

'Pleased to hear it. Sleep well.' I open my bedroom door. 'Horatio!'

'Yes.'

'Sleep well, I said.'

'Heard you.'

I put the crack in a rolled-up pair of socks in the sock drawer in the chest of drawers, then switch on the aircon and the fan. Feel clammy and my heart is still beating faster than normal. I go into the bathroom and wipe my face with a towel. I lie down on the bed, peer up at the ceiling, and listen to the hum of the aircon. There's a mosquito in here, can hear it buzzing. I pick up an A4 pad and turn on the main light. Where is it ...? Not on the ceiling, not on the walls, not under the bed, not on the chest of drawers. The buzzing has stopped. I switch off the aircon and cup a hand to my ear. Nothing ... *Bbbzzz*. I hit it with a forehand swipe. The mosquito falls to the floor and spins in circles on its side. Down comes the pad. There is blood splatter on the pad. Must have already bitten me. *Ah!* I want to kill it all over again.

The aircon's hum has mutated into voices, gossiping voices. The family's voices – Mum, her father, Genevieve. I know they are talking about my father, but can't hear what they are saying. When I switch the aircon off, I hear the tree frogs outside. They are louder than normal, much louder ... Their croaking mutates

46

into the same gossiping voices as the aircon. I wrap the pillow over my ears.

I am clammy, can't lie still, and am not sleepy. Crack will make me feel better. It isn't that late, it's eleven-fifteen. Could do it now, and still get enough sleep. Better be quiet though, Mum is next door. I creep downstairs to the kitchen and get a firelighter and a piece of tinfoil. Back in my room, I roll up a piece of paper into a cone, make the tinfoil into a bowl shape, get the crack from the chest of drawers, unwrap it, and go out onto the balcony. I am looking at the rock and wondering what smoking the whole thing in one go would feel like. Would be full-on, that's for sure. There's only one way to find out. I crouch down, put one end of the rolled-up piece of paper in my mouth, grip the tinfoil by the rim with my left hand, click the firelighter on, place it under the tinfoil, and suck. Blood rushes to my head, I drop the firelighter and tinfoil, fall back into the room, and slide the door shut with my foot. Power is surging through me, waves of power.

'Rahhhh …! Rahhhh …! RAHHHH! RAHHHHHH!'

'AHHHHH!' Mum is in the doorway. I am standing in the middle of the floor with my arms raised above my head. I lower them. Mum is staring at me. 'AHHHH!'

She races out of the room and slams the door shut. I am wasted. Power is still surging through me and I feel as if I could fly. I run in a circle around the room. I spin around and run in a circle in the opposite direction … In big trouble if they find out about the crack. What do I do? Quick, think. My heart is racing, can feel it reverberating in my ears. And I'm high, super high. But my thinking is clear, crystal clear. First thing is the smell. I dart into the bathroom, smear toothpaste on my teeth, rinse my mouth with water, and spit it out. In the mirror above the sink, I see my reflection. My eyes are the size of saucers. If they see them, it's game over. I wash my hands with soap, dry my sweaty face and neck with a towel, then return to the bedroom. Thudding footsteps are coming upstairs. I jump into bed and pull the sheet up to my chin.

The door bursts open and Mum's father strides in. He glares at me, doesn't say anything. I'm looking at him but keeping my head bowed so he doesn't see my eyes. My heart is still beating like crazy. Mum and Genevieve come in. They position themselves at the foot of the bed in a line. Mum's father in the middle, Mum on his left, Genevieve on his right. Mum is trembling, her stepmother is muttering something, and her father is glaring at me. No one says anything. Still super high, but less than before. Thank God crack only lasts a short time. They will demand to know why I was doing what I was doing. Was the roaring I think I was doing that woke Mum and made her come in. Genevieve says, 'What happened here?' *Just say it was a nightmare, must've been sleepwalking.* 'Horatio, I asked you what happened? Was awoken in my room by bellowing. Was as if it was the devil himself.'

'Son,' whispers Mum. 'Tell us what's going on?'

I keep my head bowed when I say, 'Was sleeping fine but then had this nightmare.' I cover my face with my hands. 'It was so real. Think I must've been sleepwalking.' I point at the window. 'Because woke up over there—'

'All this pandemonium,' says Genevieve, 'over a nightmare!'

Mum says, 'Let him tell us what happened.'

Should just blame it on the stress from hearing my father was shot. I say, 'Sleepwalked over there as I said. Must have.' I keep my head down. 'Mum, your shrieking woke me up.'

Mum says, 'What was the nightmare about?'

'My father.' I cover my face with my hands again. 'In the nightmare I saw what happened to him. And it was so real, not like normal dreams when I can tell straight away it's only a dream.'

Mum moves over to the side of the bed, touches my shoulder, and says, 'Can imagine, must've been terrifying.' She touches my hair. 'Your hair's wet and you're hot.'

She switches on the aircon and joins the others at the foot of the bed. Her father says, 'Just try and relax, everything will be fine.'

Genevieve says, 'You are telling us it was a nightmare that made you bellow as if you were The Devil incarnate.'

'Genevieve,' says Mum. 'Leave it.'

'Horatio,' says her father, 'how are you feeling now?'

'A bit better.'

'Good,' he says.

They whisper to each other. Mum says, 'Will be back in a minute. Okay?'

I say, 'Yes.'

They leave my room. Can hear them talking on the landing. My heart is still pounding, but not nearly as fast. Mum comes into the room; I squeeze my eyes shut. She kneels beside the bed, places her hand on my shoulder, and says, 'You're still hot and your heart is beating fast.'

'Feeling a bit better though and quite sleepy.'

'That's good, you should try to sleep. I will bring you some water.' Mum returns with a glass of water and puts it on the bedside table. 'There you go.' She kisses my forehead. 'Everything will be fine. I'm here and your grandfather is staying downstairs. There is nothing to worry about. So sorry what you went through.'

She leaves the door slightly open. The sound coming from the aircon is the usual *hum*.

*

It is 08:19, and I am still in bed. Feeling quite drowsy and kind of agitated. The firelighter, tinfoil and the rolled-up paper are still on the balcony. It wouldn't be ideal if someone found them there. I get up and go out onto the balcony. It is already pretty hot. I pick up everything, go inside, wrap the tinfoil and paper in some tissues, and put them in the bin. There is a knock on my door. Mum says, 'Good morning.'

'Morning.'

49

'Ready for some breakfast? Thinking of making omelettes.'

'Yes, I'll eat an omelette.'

'Come down when you're ready.' The hob has to be lit; she will be needing the firelighter. Best get moving. I pull on a T-shirt and some shorts and go downstairs. Mum kisses me on the cheek. 'How're you feeling?'

'Fine.'

'You slept alright then, in the end?'

'Yeah.'

Mum is whisking eggs in a bowl. I slip the firelighter into the drawer I took it from, pour myself a glass of orange juice, and sit down at the table … The omelette has cheese, ham and tomato in it. Mum says how sorry she is about the nightmare, how dreadful it must have been, and how she got the biggest shock of her life. She blows air from her mouth, and then says, 'Not the biggest shock actually. But a big shock.' She gulps water from her glass. 'You're not working in the launderette today.' *Excellent.* 'I'm supposed to be running some errands with your grandfather this morning. Are you okay with that? I can stay if not.' I nod. 'Are you sure? I'm happy to stay.'

'No, go.'

'As long as you're sure.' She puts a forkful of omelette in her mouth and swallows. 'In that case the plan is you'll be with Carlton this morning. He's going to drop his daughter with the mother. You two are going to go to the gym.'

'I can stay here on my own.'

'That is not what will be happening. It's a good opportunity for you to let off some steam.'

'Fine, whatever.'

'Hope you'll show Carlton some enthusiasm. It's kind of him to offer to take you.' Mum folds her arms. 'You weren't doing anything with Dougal last night that you shouldn't have been?'

'No.'

Several seconds have passed when she says, 'Okay.' After

breakfast, I have a quick shower, brush my teeth, get changed, and answer some probability questions from one of my maths textbooks. Mum is calling me. I go downstairs. 'We're waiting for you outside.'

She leaves the house. I put on my trainers and go outside. They are all huddled together in the courtyard – Mum, her father, Genevieve, Carlton, his daughter, and behind them, Dougal. They are all looking at me. Dougal is shifting his weight from side to side. Mum's father says, 'Good morning.' He comes over and puts his arm over my shoulders. 'How are you this fine day?'

'Okay.'

Mum says, 'I made Horatio an omelette for breakfast.'

Her father squeezes my shoulders, and says, 'Lucky boy.'

He joins the others. They are all watching me. Mum says, 'We're off.' She kisses me on the cheek. 'Have fun with Carlton. See you later.'

'Bye.'

Her father says, 'Enjoy the gym.'

They leave. Genevieve makes a huffing noise and struts off to the other house. The little girl is skipping around the courtyard. Carlton and Dougal are looking at me. Carlton says, 'Get ready. You'll need a T-shirt, shorts, towel, water.'

I go into the house, take a bottle of mineral water from the fridge, and then part the lace curtain in the living room area. Dougal is still shifting from side to side. I head upstairs, get a clean T-shirt and shorts, and shove them in the mini rucksack along with the bottle of water.

Carlton is driving, I am in the front passenger seat, his daughter is in the back. She says, 'Horatio, you like gym?'

'Yes.'

Carlton glances at me, and says, 'What training have you done?'

'Been to the gym a few times. Used the cardio machines, did sit-ups, press-ups.'

He clicks the left indicator. His daughter says, 'Daddy is the strongest daddy in the whole world.' Carlton chuckles. She is tapping the side of my seat. 'Horatio!'

'Yes.'

'Daddy carry huge weight. He lie and push up like this. Look.' I twist around in the seat. She lifts her arms above her head. 'Weeee!'

'Darling, it's called bench press.' We pull up outside a small house painted bright yellow. 'Won't be a minute.'

They walk over to the house. A woman comes out of it. She is tall, slim, and very black. That will be the mother. She has her fists on her hips. Mum does that when she is angry. Carlton returns to the car, pulls the door shut, pinches the bridge of his nose, and turns the key in the ignition.

The gym is small and dingy. It has a sign outside it – 'Exercise Empowers. Drugs Destroy.' It is quite dirty inside and there is no hi-tech equipment just weights, a couple of pull-up bars, and a boxing bag. I start off with some stretching. Carlton tells me he doesn't want to see me trying to lift anything heavy, as I haven't done weights before and am still young. He does weight training with another man; I do some squats and lunges. Carlton started off bench pressing light weights. He has now ramped it up to one hundred and sixty kilograms. People have gathered around the bench. As he pumps reps, they clap and cheer. His daughter might be right, Carlton could be the strongest daddy in the world. My father would have been strong and athletic like me. Not as big and strong as Carlton, but faster and fitter than him. I do five sets of seven pull-ups with one minute rest between each. My biceps and forearms feel pumped. Now Carlton is dead lifting. It doesn't look much fun in this heat. He lowers the bar and calls out to me, 'Do some boxing.'

Why not? I punch a boxing bag hanging from the ceiling. A man tells me to put gloves on. I put some on. Will be more fun if I imagine it's not a boxing bag, but somebody I hate. Mum's dead boyfriend – Fool's Gold … He is grinning at me with his mouth open, showing his fool's gold-capped front tooth. *Bam* – that was a direct hit. The tooth flies out of his mouth along with a jet of blood. *Bam, bam.* Fool's Gold topples backwards unconscious. When I climb up onto the ropes on the side of the ring, the crowd cheer. Next up is the psychiatrist Mum sent me to in London. Nightmare she was. People say you shouldn't hit women. Well, I am going to lay a beating on this one. I stun her with a left jab to the tip of the nose, then smash her with a right uppercut under the chin, which lifts her up off the ground. The referee doesn't even bother counting, just calls for a stretcher.

Serena and Dalilah are strutting around the ring in bathing suits, holding up cards with Round One written on them. I am leaning on the ropes with my arms draped over them. My opponent is Javel. I hit him with two left hooks to the head and he crashes to the floor. Mouthguard is half out of his mouth and his eyes are in the back of his head. Now it's the policeman's turn; the one who searched me at the bus stop. He walks straight into a right cross.

Nearly as hot as the launderette in here. I take off the gloves and gulp water from the bottle I brought with me. The man who gave me the gloves comes over, and says, 'Pad work, gloves on.' I put the gloves on. 'Stand more side on. Less of a target that way. Left hand a bit higher … Left jab.' I do a left jab. 'Faster … Another … That's it … Right cross.' Carlton is watching me. 'Jab, cross, left hook, right upper cut … Keep the hook tighter.' He demonstrates. 'Again … One more time.' He lowers the pads and says to Carlton, 'Fast hands this white relative of yours.'

'Seeing that.' Carlton chuckles. 'Renaming him The Antiguan Mayweather.'

FIVE

O8:10 – MONDAY – Mum is driving me to school in her father's dented Toyota. She didn't want me to go there by bus like I normally do. She didn't say why. School starts at eight-thirty, and we're not even in St. John's yet.

'You have cricket practice this afternoon. Your grandfather will drive you back afterwards.' *Whatever.* This slow lorry has been in front of us for ages. Finally, it swerves off the road onto a building site. Mum accelerates. 'Really worried about Tanice.' She presses the indicator and turns right. 'We have to brace ourselves for the worst.' Mum is biting on her lower lip. She does not say what the worst is. 'How are you feeling?'

'Fine.'

'Are you sure?'

'Yes.'

'You slept okay last night?'

'Yeah.'

'All the way through?'

'Yes.'

She strokes my shoulder, and says, 'Pleased to hear it. Now I know I didn't handle the situation regarding your father as well as I might have.'

'You didn't!'

'*Okay.*' She grips the steering wheel tightly. We have arrived.

She pats my leg. 'Love you. Have a good day, see you this evening.'

The first class of the day is maths. Today's topic is quadratic algebraic equations. They are a type of polynomial equation, as they consist of two or more algebraic terms. The highest power for a quadratic equation is two. The teacher writes on the white board, $ax2 + bx + c = 0$. This is the standard quadratic equation formula. He turns to face the class.

'In this quadratic equation A and B are coefficients. Cornelius, can you tell us what C is?'

'Don't know, Sir.'

C is the constant term.

'Garfield?'

'C is the number on its own. It is labelled the constant term.'

'Correct.'

The next class is religious education. I am sitting in the back row. Today, the priest who did the service at the cathedral is giving a talk. *Boring.*

'Every day you come to school you see the sign outside – *Drugs End All Dreams.*' He is holding his left index finger up at shoulder height. 'This is because it is vitally important to your future. This lesson must be implanted in your hearts and brains ... One only has to see how drugs have ravaged our society.' I open my maths textbook under the desk. 'Take a walk around here and you will find addicts aplenty. Their sordid existences are mired by hopelessness, squalor, and the absence of The Lord ...'

$x2 + 5x + 6 = 0$

$x2 + 2x + 3x + 6 = 0$

$x(x + 2) + 3(x + 2) = 0$

$(x + 2)(x + 3) = 0$

'One Peter, Chapter Five, verse eight. Be alert and of sober mind. Your enemy the devil prowls around like a roaring lion looking for someone to devour.' *The two obtained factors of the quadratic equation are (x + 2) and (x + 3).* 'Proverbs 22:3. The prudent see danger and take refuge, but the simple keep going and pay the penalty.'

*

I tap the base of the cricket bat on the ground and wait for the ball. Here it comes. I move the bat forward. The ball comes off the side of it and sails into the net on my right. That would have got me one run. The bowler calls out, 'Caught in the slips.'

'No, would have got a run off that.'

'Caught all day.'

In the net next to mine, Garfield says, 'You'd be out unless the fielder had flippers for hands.'

I will hit the next ball for a four, or even a six. They won't be able to argue with that. Mum's father has arrived. The bowler says, 'Garfield, bowl him a leggy.'

'Coming up.'

Garfield is rubbing the ball against his trouser leg. He runs forward and bowls. I watch the ball as it flies through the air. It bounces off the ground a couple of feet in front of me and veers right. I hit the ball hard and it smashes into the top of the net. That's at least a four, maybe even a six. Mum's father is clapping … Cricket practice is over. I collect my stuff and walk over to him. He slaps me on the shoulder, and says, 'Great shot that was. Smooth technique.'

He takes my mini rucksack off me. It has my schoolbooks in. I carry my sports bag with my school clothes in to his car. The dent has gone. I say, 'You got the car repaired.'

He slaps the side of the car and says, 'Carlton's crew knocked it into shape.'

We get in and drive off … This is not the normal route. Why is he driving this way? He parks in front of a row of businesses on the edge of town and tells me we are here to get some help with my problem. We go into a doctor's surgery. A female doctor asks

56

about my nightmare and the sleep walking. I tell her it was a one off, and that I slept well on Saturday night and last night. Mum's father says, 'And that's fantastic. However, we can't just forget how bad you were on Friday night. It was extremely concerning for everyone.'

The doctor asks me how I'm feeling now. I'm thinking she is going to prescribe me pills; pills that I don't want or need. But after talking to Mum's father for a while, she says as it was a one off there is no need to prescribe pills. She tells me to come back if I have more issues with my sleep.

I say, 'Okay.'

Mum's father says, 'He most certainly will.'

When we arrive, Mum comes out of the other house, and says, 'We're speaking to Tanice on the phone. Dump your stuff and come straight over.'

Ah! I drink a glass of water, stuff my sweaty cricket clothes in the washing machine, sit down for a minute, and then go to the other house. Mum is on the sofa in the living room with her chin resting on her hands. Her father is walking back and forth across the room with a phone pressed to his ear.

'Hold on in there. We're all praying for you … Love you.'

He passes the phone to Mum, sighs, bows his head, and leaves the room. Mum says, 'Me again, Sis. Wish I was there with you … Shaneeka's coming to see you on Wednesday. Fingers crossed for those tests … Have someone here who wants a word with you.' *I don't.* 'Stay strong. Bye for now.'

She gives me the phone and collapses onto the sofa. I hold the phone to my ear, and say, 'Hello.' The line goes dead. Aunt Fatso hung up on me. Mum is peering up at me. Don't want her to know her fat sister hung up on me. Mum will want to know why, and she might even try and blame me for it. Easiest thing is just pretend I am speaking to her. 'Good luck with those tests … Oh, Shaneeka is coming to visit you in hospital. When …? Wednesday, nice … Bye.'

Mum says, 'How did she sound to you?'

'Normal.'

'Sounded frail to me.'

Mum starts sobbing. I say, 'What are we having for dinner?'

'Haven't thought about dinner!' *Sniff.* 'Have other things on my mind other than food. I want to talk with your grandfather now, please go to the other house.'

In the other house, I get the iPad from the living room area and go up to my room. The UK is four hours ahead of Antigua. This could be a good time to call Serena, as she won't have gone to bed yet. I open *WhatsApp* and find her number …

'Hey Horatio, how's things?'

'Not too bad. Your video is turned off.'

'*Yeah*, cos it's quite late here. I'm in my pyjamas. Tired and not looking my best.'

'Turn the video on!'

'Okay, relax.'

Serena is propped up in bed. She is covered up to her chest with a duvet, and her long, silky blonde hair is trailing down her arms.

'You have amazing hair.'

'I know.' Serena slants forward. 'You don't look as brown as I thought you would. It's sunny there, right, like all the time?'

'Yeah, a lot of the time. Haven't been outside all that much though.'

'*Hello*, you're in the Caribbean. That means sunbathing on the beach, drinking cocktails, doing water sports. That's what they do out there, know that, my friend goes to Antigua all the time.'

'People on holiday, yeah. I go to school and work in a launderette.'

'Launderette?'

'Yes, launderette.'

'Eeew!'

'Yeah. On Saturdays I work in this launderette my mum's father owns.'

'That sucks bigtime.'

'It does.'

'Nothing much happening here. It's raining like non-stop. Went shopping with Mum on the weekend, got loads of new clothes ... School is *so* boring ... Wish you were here.' She flicks a length of silky blonde hair off her face. 'Other than school and the launderette, what have you been doing?'

'I smoked crack.'

Serena holds the fingers of her left hand to her mouth. The fingernails are painted bright pink.

'No way!'

'Yeah, smoked it with my cousin.'

'What's it like?'

'Full-on.'

'Bet it is. Your cousin is turning you into a bad boy, a Caribbean gangster.'

'We just thought we'd try crack to see what it was like.'

'Crazy! You were a maths whiz when you left London, and now you're into the hardest drug out there.'

'I'm still a maths whiz. Have become an expert on Venn diagrams—'

'Don't say those words again, or I'm hanging up.' She pulls the duvet up to her chin. 'They are the most boring things ever. How's your mum?'

'She's sort of stressing out because her sister is ill.'

'Oh, your bossy aunt. Is it Covid?'

'No, cancer.'

'Oh my God, your poor mum. She only just moved to Antigua and this happens. Do you think she will return to England?'

'Not sure. Doubt it.'

We talk for a while. Then Serena says, 'Lovely talking to you.' She kisses the screen. '*Bye.*'

*

59

Saturday morning – After stuffing a heap of tablecloths and napkins in a washing machine, I look at the sheet of paper on the bench that I printed out last night at the other house. It has factorisation problems on it. $4(x + y)^2 - 28(x^2 - y^2) + 49(x^2 - y^2)^2$ ... The answer is $(9y - 5x)^2$.

A washing machine cycle has finished. I open the machine, shove my arms inside, haul out the clean laundry, trudge over to a drying machine, dump it in, and switch it on. The clothes belong to two female tourists who were here earlier. This launderette is mostly for businesses, but customers, tourists mostly, sometimes wander in. The two tourists looked like druggies. The manager was here when they came, so didn't ask if they wanted to buy anything. She has gone out. If she's still out when they come to collect their clothes, I will ask them. I do a punch combination in the air – jab, jab, right cross, left hook, right uppercut. I pivot ninety degrees and repeat the combo. Next up – jab, left hook, right uppercut, a step back, and a right cross. *Bam, bam, bam,* step back, and *bam.* I do it again. The first three punches are all about speed; the right cross is the knockout blow. For the right cross, I bend my knees to get maximum power. Last night I hit the punchbag in Carlton's yard and did some pad work with him. He lives five minutes' walk away from where I'm staying. His punches are super hard, but slow. Mine are fast.

Before the manager left, she told me to press a stack of table-cloths. The press has two long plates, which are cushioned on the inside. I unlock the press, open it, switch on the power, select the temperature on the dial, and pull down on the lever. The fabric needs to be damp, and this tablecloth isn't. I use the spray bottle to dampen it. Am trying to remember what my father looked like. There are no photos of him at home in London. Mum surely has some photos of him somewhere ... It's all in the technique. Keep the hands moving backwards and forwards. Keep the material at the back of the press and bring it forward section by section. Tablecloths and sheets need to be folded in four.

Five tablecloths done, and they are perfect. Even the Royal Family would eat off these. Time for another combination – jab, left hook to the head, step back, right cross to the body, right uppercut to the chin. I do it slowly to get the technique exactly right … And now at full speed. *Bam, bam*, step back, *bam, bam*. And again. *Bam, bam*, step back, *bam—*

'*HI!*' The two tourists are standing in the entrance. They are white, quite young, and skanky looking. I wipe my face with a towel and go over to them. 'Were you doing boxing?'

'Yeah.'

The one who just spoke has rank, matted dreadlocks. She must take drugs. The other one says, 'Are our clothes ready yet?'

'Almost. Three or four minutes away.'

'Awesome.'

They come inside. The tourist with the rank dreadlocks says, 'You're not from here, you're from the UK, right? Can tell by your accent.'

'Yes, London.'

'I'm from Luton.'

'Never been.'

'You're not missing much.'

'I'm from Canada,' says the other one. *Not interested.* 'We're staying near the beach.'

She extends a dirty looking finger in the direction of the beach. Her friend says, 'How come you ended up working in an Antiguan launderette?'

'I was unlucky.' They laugh. 'Living out here as have family here.'

'Must suck dude,' says the Canadian. 'Everyone being here on holiday and you're working in a launderette.'

'Yeah, it sucks bigtime.' The drying machine with their stuff in has stopped spinning. 'Your clothes are ready.' They follow me through the launderette to the drying machine. The Canadian opens it and shovels the clothes into a bin liner. Right, time to get to the point. 'Do you two party?'

61

'Sure,' says the English one. 'Who doesn't?'

'Are you after anything?'

The Canadian stops shovelling the clothes, peers up at me, and says, 'So, you're a bad boy?'

'Come to think of it,' says the English one, 'we could do with something. We're going to a beach party tonight. You should come.'

The Canadian stands up, and says, 'Aren't you a bit young to be pushing?'

'Was just asking, wasn't pushing.'

They step away from me and whisper to each other. The English one says, 'We're after coke. Can you get it?'

'Sure can.'

I take their phone number and tell them I will phone when I finish here. They haven't been gone long when a van arrives to collect clean bed linen. I lug bags down to the van and shove them in the back. The van drives off. My phone *beeps*. It is a text from Mum, asking me how my day is going. I walk up the steps to the porch. Am about to go inside when I see Javel loping along the side of the road, heading towards the track that runs alongside the launderette. The idiot tried to get me in trouble with the police. Must have been him. When he passes the launderette, I call out, 'Know it was you!'

He stops, snarls, holds his middle finger up at me, and calls out, 'White bwoy!'

'You ratted on me. You are a rat; you even look like a rat.'

'Chupitness.' *Means nonsense, know that.* 'Hush!'

'No, I won't. You tried to get me in trouble but you failed, Rat Boy.' He strides over to the steps leading up to the porch and says something in Creole. 'You're jealous because you're an ugly loser. Women hate you.'

'Fuck you!'

He retracts his head and spits a mouthful of gob. I jump back. The gob lands on the porch's wooden floor.

'Disgusting.'

'Kiss me rass!'

Can guess what that means. Jab, cross should do it. He gobs again; I move to the side.

'Retarded pankoot.'

'Kill you!'

He steps onto the steps. The manager's car pulls up. She tumbles out of it, and shrieks, 'Away with you, dunce. Or I'm calling the police.'

'Highty tiety swaaty scunt!' He points his right and middle index fingers at me, and goes, 'Bang! Bang!'

He lopes off and disappears onto the track. The manager comes up to the porch, and says, 'Don't you be mocking that boy. Stay well away from him, he could be dangerous. Don't want any trouble here, you hear me?'

'Yeah, I hear you.'

'The collection came?'

'Yes.'

'And you pressed them tablecloths?'

'Yes. What does swaaty mean?'

'Overweight. Okay?'

Makes sense. We go inside. A washing machine has completed its cycle. I transfer the load to a drying machine and switch it on. It's twelve-thirty, time for my lunchbreak. I am meeting Dalilah. I go onto the porch. Here she comes, skipping along the side of the road. She is wearing lilac-coloured thigh length shorts and her hair is tied in pigtails. She is waving at me; I wave back. We walk to the shack shop together. I buy some apples, a can of Coca-Cola and two Snickers. One of the Snickers is for her. Mum is ringing me. I don't answer. Dalilah wraps her arm around mine and tilts her face towards me.

'You have amazing hazel eyes, they're one of your best features ... Flowers are my favourite things in the world. Loved them since I was little. They are so pure.' I have a gulp of Coca-Cola.

63

'Antigua has wonderful flowers … Love frangipani especially. We have so many varieties here.' I have a bite of Snickers. 'My dream is to be a florist and to travel to all the best places in the world for flowers. Holland, Paris …' Dalilah pulls on my arm. 'Are you listening?'

'Yes, you're talking about flowers, wanting to be a florist, and going to places famous for flowers. Holland, Paris.'

'That's one of the things I like about you, you actually listen, unlike the boys here … What job do you want to do?'

'Haven't decided yet. Definitely something using maths.'

'You are brilliant at maths, know that.' *Yeah.* 'Have you been studying anything interesting at school?'

'Quadratic algebraic equations.'

'Heard of them, but don't know what they are.'

'Quadratic algebraic equations are equations that contain terms up to x two. Highest power for a quadratic equation is two …'

'You're so smart. Boys here wouldn't know about quadratic algebraic equations.'

'Javel certainly wouldn't.'

Dalilah *tuts.* The manager is on the launderette's porch. She says, 'You're looking so pretty today.'

'Oh, thank you, that's so kind of you to say.'

When we go up to the porch the manager takes out a packet of sweets, and says, 'Sweetie?'

'Yes please.' Dalilah takes one, unwraps it and pops it in her mouth. 'Delicious.' She pecks me on the cheek, says, 'Bye,' and skips off.

On the roadside, she turns and waves. The manager says, 'Prettiest girl on the island. A shining star.'

I help myself to a sweet … It's baking hot in here, too hot for boxing combos. When I have a spare moment between tasks, will do some maths. The manager comes out of the office, and says, 'Call for you.'

She passes me a phone. I hold to it my ear, and say, 'Hello.'

'Horatio.' *Mum.* 'Are you okay? You didn't respond to my text or answer when I phoned.'

'Been busy, I'm working.'

'Is everything alright?'

'Yeah.'

'Great. Come straight home after work please.'

No, I need to get the drugs for those tourists. 'Mum, I want to have a walk on the beach opposite after I finish here, as been stuck inside all day.'

'Fine, but don't take too long. And answer your phone if I ring.'

It is five-thirty. The manager locks up and says, 'Well done today. You're a good worker. You don't kick up a fuss about toiling in the heat, you just get on with it, unlike that cousin of yours, Dougal. Pulled up late near on every day. Was round the back of the launderette half the time. No prizes for guessing what he was doing. And don't get me started on his pressing. There's a reason it's called pressing and not scalding.'

She waddles off to her car. I stay on the porch. The sun disappears behind the trees on the other side of the road. The drug dealer is in, I just texted him. I text the tourists and tell them to meet me on the track behind the launderette in fifteen minutes. I don't want to be dealing drugs on the main road just in case the police come. The light is starting to fade. When I arrive, the dealer's dog growls at me from behind the yard's fence. The dealer comes staggering up to the gate, knocks his fist against mine, and says, 'Wah gwaan, Redmem.'

'Redmem?'

'Light complexion.' He opens the gate. 'Enter.' I follow him to the shack. The dog is still growling at me. 'Shout sickum 'n he'll kill you.' Inside, there is a woman in a filthy lime green T-shirt slouched on a shabby sofa smoking off tinfoil. She reels backwards and stares at me with bulging eyes. Her mouth is hanging open; she is missing a lot of teeth. I quite need a piss. Don't want to ask to use his bathroom though, as it will be rank. 'Powder or rock?'

'Two grammes of powder.'

I give him the money and he gives me two tiny transparent plastic seal bags with white powder in. When I open the front door, he says, 'Pankoot, dawg'll eat you alive.'

He comes with me to the gate and punches my fist. I put the drugs in my pocket. Through the only window in Javel's shack, I can see a light on. I make my way through the shanty to the track. A mosquito lands on my forearm. I squash it and flick it away. The light is fading fast and it won't be long until the tree frogs start croaking. A warm breeze coming from the sea brushes against my face. A van with its headlights on is coming up the track. It drives past me. A couple of seconds later it beeps its horn. What was it beeping at? There are no vehicles behind me. If there were, I would hear them and see the headlights. Those skanks should be here by now.

Close behind me I hear a crunching sound, as if someone stepped on a gravelly bit of the path. In the side-view mirror of a beat-up car parked on the side of the track, I see the outline of someone. I lower myself to one knee, reach down as if I'm doing up my shoelace, and look over my shoulder. Someone is coming towards me. They are holding something in their right hand at shoulder height. I dash right and go around the side of the beat-up car. An object is flying through the air. I bow my head. It sails over me and lands in the undergrowth. Must have been a rock.

'White bwoy!' Javel followed me. He is on the other side of the car. Something splatters on the roof. Must be gob. He is bent over, probably picking up another rock. I hurdle over the bonnet. He stands up and brings his right arm back. 'Murda you!' I throw a jab which lands on the tip of his nose. 'Mahh!' He drops the rock he is holding and lashes out at me with a wild left hook. I lean back as his fist flies through the air in front of my face. He jerks to the side and I throw a right cross to his head. He collapses to his knees. 'Mahh!'

'Oh my God!'

That was the Canadian tourist. I kick Javel in the side; he topples over.

'Leave him!'

That was the woman with the skanky dreadlocks. Javel groans and gets up on all fours. A kick to the ribs sends him down again.

'Get away from him!'

Skanky Hair is tugging on my arm. I pull myself free and stand over Javel. He turns onto his front and starts pushing himself up with his arms. I shove my right foot on his lower back, and say, 'Loser. You're older than me, but you didn't last two seconds.'

'Fuck you!'

I am going to drench him in piss; that will teach him a lesson. I press down harder with my foot. The Canadian screeches, 'Enough!'

I pull out my cock. A jet of urine splashes onto his head and neck. Javel shrieks, 'MAHHH!'

'Oh my God!' screeches the Canadian.

'*NO!*' screams Skanky Hair.

Javel crawls out from under my foot, clambers to his feet, and rushes off up the track. I pull my shorts up. The Canadian screeches, 'Why did you do it?' She starts crying. 'Wahh! Wahh!'

They hurry off down the track and disappear into the darkness. Skanky Hair comes back, and says, 'Did you get it?'

'Yeah.'

I give her the drugs. She shoves some crumpled banknotes in my palm, says, 'You're gross,' and hurries off.

She must be referring to her hair. I go to the road and wait for the bus.

*

When I get back to the house, Mum is slouched at the table downstairs with her head in her hands. She looks up at me. Her eyes are red. Has she been smoking ganja?

'How was the launderette?'

'Boiling hot and hard work.'

'Went to the beach this afternoon for a walk with your grandfather.' *And?* 'On another subject, how have you been sleeping?'

'Pretty well.'

'No more nightmares?'

'No, none.'

'Good. What happened to your right hand?' The knuckle is cut and there's blood on it. 'Show me!' I put my hand flat on the table. 'What happened?'

'Was doing a boxing combination at the launderette and punched the wall.'

'Be careful. Don't want you hurting yourself or breaking a machine. Stay there.' In the kitchen area, Mum rummages in a cupboard and pulls out a first aid kit. She wipes disinfectant on the cut and puts a plaster on it. 'All patched up. What're you going to do now?'

'Might see what Dougal is up to.'

Her eyes sort of narrow. She says, 'Okay, you can do that I suppose. Are you hungry?'

'Quite.'

'There's a bit of sushi and a chocolate bar for you in the fridge.'

Mum goes up to her room. There isn't much sushi, little more than a starter. Tastes alright though. The chocolate is a rock-hard Snickers. It's too hot here to keep chocolate anywhere else other than in the fridge. After eating, I phone Dougal. He doesn't answer. Presumably stoned and hasn't even noticed his phone is ringing. I haven't smoked anything since the night on the crack. Wouldn't mind a smoke; there's not much else to do. I head over to Dougal's. There is no answer when I knock on the door. Am about to leave when he comes through the front gate carrying a plastic bag. He sighs, and says, 'Wa gwaan, Cuz?'

'Not a lot. Was working in the launderette all day.'

'Dat's no fun.' He unlocks the front door and goes inside. I go in too. He takes food from the bag and puts it in the fridge and in cupboards. 'Will have a spliff with you, but dat's it. Doing my own thing dis evening. Better not have any crack with you.'

'I don't.'

'Nearly had a heart attack when I heard you'd gone crazy dat night. Thought it was all about to blow up. Crabs times ten ... 'N from now on you use eye whitener drops before you leave. Got some here. Don't want your mother blaming me for being a bad influence on her precious son.' He sighs. 'Other way around. Always has been.'

He rolls and lights a spliff. I don't particularly want to be in my room this evening, as not in the mood for doing maths, reading, or using the iPad. Could go to that beach party those tourists mentioned for an hour or two. Think Dougal has a motorbike.

'There's a party at the beach near the launderette.'

'Jolly Beach.'

'Yes. Met these two women tourists at the launderette today. They said I should come along.'

He blows smoke from his mouth, and says, 'Hot dese women?'

'No, wretched skanks.'

Dougal splutters. Smoke comes out of his nose. He says, 'Cuz, you're really selling dis party to me.'

He passes me the spliff. I inhale on it, exhale, and say, 'There will be other women and girls there.'

'No doubt.'

He doesn't seem that interested. More persuading is required. How about, 'McDonald's Dalilah is going to be there. She's been trying to pull her jeans on all day. She's finally succeeded, and she's ready to party.'

'Hah, you're funny Cuz, will give you dat.'

'How about going for a few hours?'

69

'Nah, risk is too big.'

'There's no risk.'

'Dere is. You! You're volatile. Seem cool now. When we get dere though, you could be smoking off tinfoil 'n doing your sadist shit with animals, or party goers. Cuz, you're a menace to society.'

I can't go alone, the buses stop soon, and I won't be able to get back here. I say, 'Come on.'

'No way! Not so soon after dat shit you pulled.'

'Didn't do anything wrong.'

'Dat's it, I'm done.' He stubs the spliff out. 'Take dese.' He passes me a bottle of eyedrops. 'Drop in each eye. Keep dem, you'll be needing dem.'

I leave. Mum has sent a text.

....

Today 19:41

Popping out 4 a bit. Won't be late. Want you back here by 10 latest. Your grandfather's in if you need anything. Be good. Mum X

....

I am walking up the track. It is a clear night and the stars are out. The stars are distinct over here, not like in London where if they appear at all, they are blurry. A light directly above my head is blinking. Must be a satellite. I push open the gate, squeeze inside, and close it behind me. Have taken a couple of steps into the courtyard when I hear in the other house Mum's stepmother shriek, 'That boy!' Might well be me she is talking about. I tiptoe over to the house, sidle along the wall, and peek through the living room's mosquito screen. She is in there with Mum's father. 'Listen! He could cause us trouble, big trouble.'

70

'I'm listening. And I'm sitting just here, so no need to shout.'

'A big responsibility it would be.'

'Aware of that.' *What are they talking about?* 'Seems it could be the best solution though. Nothing's settled yet.'

'Could be a big problem that boy without his mother here. He's a big problem already; but he could be a bigger problem is what I'm saying. We have witnessed his strange behaviour. You forget that already?'

'He had a nightmare, poor kid. It's been a big upheaval for him hearing the truth about his father. Imagine how you would feel.'

'Bellowing he was, as if he were The Devil incarnate.'

'Don't be starting on that nonsense again.'

'That boy—'

'That boy is my grandson. His name is Horatio. Always treated your son Carlton as one of my own, and here you are treating my flesh and blood like an outsider.'

'Carlton was never any trouble despite being big enough to cause plenty.'

'True. But my grandson hasn't caused any trouble either, has he?'

'That's as maybe.'

'Enough!'

'You're not taking on board what I'm saying.'

'Listen to me. Tanice is gravely ill. She is over there with not much in the way of family. Her mother is all the way up in the north of the country, and she wouldn't be of much use anyway. Can't deal with anything stressful, never could. Other than her it's only my granddaughter, and she's away at college. Fair way away from London it is too. Rakesha can stay at Tanice's house and visit her every day at the hospital. Depending on how things work out, she'll bring Horatio over. That's if she feels the situation is such that she can't return. She'd never just dump her son. It would be a short-term thing … Will be flying over there myself at some point.'

71

So, Mum is thinking of returning to England because her fat sister is ill and might die. If it happens, I will have the whole house to myself. Otherwise, it will be much the same as now.

SIX

THE FOLLOWING FRIDAY – I am on my way back from school. The bus stops and people get off. Some of them are from my school. One of them is Cornelius. As he disembarks, he says, 'Horatio, have a good weekend.'

Some people get on and the bus drives off. I am looking at my English literature homework. There are three questions. The first is, *How does Charlotte Brontë incorporate elements of the Gothic tradition into Jane Eyre?* Easy. I take an A4 pad from my mini rucksack, put it on my lap, and start writing. *The structure of the text in the Gothic literary tradition is supposed to* ... summon. No, call forth ... Evoke – that's the word I'm looking for ... *Oftentimes this is achieved through supernatural elements, mystery, and secrets. One of the ways Charlotte Brontë does this is by emphasising the Gothic aspects of Thornfield Hall.*

While I think what else to write, I look out of the window. There are lots of tourists on the side of the road, coming and going from the beach. Through the trees beside the road, I can see the sea. It could be described as a resplendent blue. Has been a searing hot day and tourists just can't get enough of the heat. Fair few of them are lobster red. Those three young women look like partygoers. Say they bought two grammes each, that would be an easy sixty EC. There is a middle-aged man with a paunch and a straw hat drinking a bottle of beer. Probably suffering from what

73

is called midlife crisis. May well have just bought a sports car and is chasing young girls he's too old to get. That's assuming he ever could in the first place. Wouldn't take long to persuade him to buy a gramme, or two.

And those three eighteen, nineteen-year-old boys carrying tennis rackets and wearing white tennis clothes look like perfect targets. They'll be up for partying, and they'll have rich parents to pay for it. Three grammes there. I could have just earned a minimum of one hundred and eighty EC. Would take near on twenty-six hours to earn that much in the launderette. The teacher was discussing in class on Tuesday *Jane Eyre's* Gothic theme. I tap my pen against my thigh as I remember what he said … That was it. Brontë employs the Gothic elements to increase the emotion and tension. She also uses it to reveal an almost supernatural connection between Jane Eyre and Mr Rochester … Done. Next question.

Back at the house I have a snack, learn some Spanish vocabulary for school, and when it has cooled down a bit, go to Carlton's, use the punch bag in his garden, do some press-ups and sit-ups, and then return to the house. Mum makes pasta with a tomato sauce for dinner. It's not bad, but the sauce is a bit sweet. It was imported from the US. They love their sugar over there. After dinner, I read for a while and play games on the iPad. Am about to fall asleep when I hear Mum and her father talking in the courtyard. It is nearly midnight. Usually, they would be in bed by now. Maybe something has happened. I go downstairs. Through the mosquito screen on the window, I can see their outlines. Mum says, 'How could such a thing happen?'

'No idea, darling. Tomorrow we'll know more. It's out, and that's the main thing.'

'Ouch, mosquito! Let's go inside.'

They are going to the other house. What were they talking about?

*

The next morning – 'HORATIO!' That is Mum shrieking from downstairs. I roll onto my side and pick my watch off the bedside table. 07:09. My shift at the launderette doesn't start till nine. Don't need to get up yet. I can hear her coming upstairs. She knocks on my door. 'Get up please.'

'No, staying in bed. Not starting work till—'

'Something's happened. Get up, get ready. You're leaving soon.'

Ah! What's happened and what's it got to do with me? I get up, get changed, and go downstairs. Mum hands me a glass of orange juice. 'They're waiting for you in the car.' She gives me two apples. 'To eat on the way.' She kisses me on the cheek. 'See you later.'

I've got my hat, sunglasses, and some cash just in case anyone is after anything. The Toyota is parked outside the courtyard's gate. Mum's father and Carlton are in the front, Dougal is in the back. I get in and we drive off. Mum's father says, 'Was an incident last night at the launderette.'

'What happened?'

'A fire. Not sure exactly what occurred yet, it was too dark last night to tell much. Fair bit of damage though. Need your help clearing up the mess.'

Wonder what caused the fire. Could have been an electrical fire, what with all the washing and drying machines in there. Guess I won't be working there until the damage is repaired. We park outside the launderette. Sections of the entrance are completely burnt away, and I can see through them into the launderette. The front of the building is black and there is a hole in the middle of the porch. It smells of burnt wood. A car arrives and a man wearing a white shirt and grey trousers gets out of it. He speaks with Mum's father on an undamaged part of the porch. Dougal and Carlton are chatting on the roadside. I stay at the bottom of the launderette's steps, so I can hear what is being discussed. Mum's father says, 'You're saying it's arson?'

75

'Was deliberate, that much is obvious. The door and porch were doused with a flammable liquid.'

'But why? This is a friendly community. And no one has a vendetta against me. I am friends with everyone.'

The man strokes his chin and says, 'What I can tell you is whoever did this made a right mess of it. They got the flammable liquid all over the door and the porch, but not inside. If you were planning to burn the place down, you'd be wanting the fire inside. You'd smash one of those tiny windows at the back of the launderette and pour the fuel through it. The air from outside would fan the flames. Whole place would burn down in no time. Whoever did this is a halfwit of an arsonist.'

Javel. They go inside. They are in there for a few minutes. Then the man gets in his car and drives off. Mum's father says, 'Let's get this mess cleared up.'

Carlton gets some tools from the boot of the Toyota. He uses a thin metal bar to pry off the planks from the porch. Me and Dougal carry the planks down the steps and put them in a pile in the scrub between the launderette and the track. The neighbours have congregated around Mum's father. I hear one of them say, 'Was awakened by a godawful shriek coming from here.'

Another says, 'Proper inferno it was. Hose couldn't stretch this far, so we filled buckets with water and threw them on the blaze.'

'I am so grateful, thank you. You saved my business from worse damage.' Me and Dougal go up the steps to the launderette, pick up a partially burnt length of wood, and carry it down the steps. 'Who would do such a thing?'

A woman says, 'One or two vagabonds up there might.' She is flapping her hand in the direction of the shanty at the top of the track. 'They are causing all sorts of mischief.'

Mum's father says, 'But why would they do it? I didn't cause them no bother.'

'Drugs,' says the woman.

'If they wanted money for drugs, why would they burn my launderette? No money in that.'

'Cos the drugs drive them crazy.'

Me and Dougal put the length of wood we are carrying with the rest of the burnt wood. Dougal is looking at me. I say, 'What?'

'Am thinking is what.'

The wood from the porch has all been cleared, and Carlton is now ripping off the remnants of the door. I help nail a plywood board where the door was, so the place is secure. The manager has arrived. Mum's father has one arm over her shoulders and she is hugging him around the waist. I hear her say, 'Why would someone cause this wanton destruction?' I carry some tools to the car. 'Good morning, Horatio.'

'Good morning.'

I put the tools in the boot. The manager is watching me and biting on a fingernail. Have just gone up to the porch when a police pickup truck pulls up behind the Toyota. A policeman gets out. It is the policeman who searched me at the bus stop. He is talking with Mum's father. The clear-up operation is finished and Carlton and Dougal are sitting on the launderette's steps. I am sitting on the step above them. Most of the people have left. The policeman is still talking with Mum's father. Carlton passes me an open bottle of mineral water. I have a glug and pass it back to him. They are coming this way. We move to the side. The policeman says, 'Good morning.'

We say, 'Good morning.'

The policeman stops and stares at me. His eyes have narrowed into slits and his tongue is stuck in his cheek. He and Mum's father go to the far end of the porch. Mum's father says, 'Think there's much chance of catching the fool who did this?'

'Neighbours said they heard a godawful shriek. Stands to reason whoever did this hurt themselves and that's why they were shrieking. Something to go on there.'

Dalilah has showed up. She is waving at me from the roadside. Dougal says, 'Dat's Dalilah.'

Carlton blows air from his mouth, and says, 'Wow!'

When I go over to her, she says, 'Heard about the fire. Someone lit it on purpose is what people are saying.' She peers up at the launderette. 'How is it inside?'

'Not too bad, there's only damage in the entrance area.'

As the policeman walks down the steps, he glares at me. He gets in the pickup truck and drives off. Dalilah tugs on my arm.

'He was eyeballing you.'

Mum's father is talking with Carlton, Dougal and the manager on the launderette's steps. Dalilah turns her back to them and whispers, 'Think Javel did it?'

I shrug my shoulders and say, 'Maybe.'

'He don't like you, know that. But it's not your business, you just work there.' She purses her lips. 'Can't think who else would do such a thing.'

They are coming this way. Mum's father slaps me on the shoulder and says, 'Good job clearing up.' The manager is talking with Dalilah. 'My suggestion is you make the best of the morning, go to the beach, and do something fun before it gets too hot. You and Dougal should rent a kayak.'

I say, 'Sure.'

'Dougal!'

'Can't, got some errands to run.'

'The errands can wait. Go with your cousin and rent kayaks for a few hours. Will be a good workout for you both.' Dougal doesn't say anything. Mum's father slaps some banknotes onto Dougal's palm. 'Get one each, more fun that way.'

Dougal says, 'Alright.'

'What do mean alright? You mean thank you.'

'Thank you.'

I say thank you. Mum's father speaks with the manager and Dalilah. He says to Dalilah, 'Appreciate your concern, young lady. We'll get the place up and running again in no time, don't you worry about that.' He says goodbye to her and the manager, comes over to me, slaps me on the shoulder again, and mutters, 'Dalilah is a very fine young lady.' And now at normal volume, 'Carlton, we're off. Long day ahead.' He punches his palm. 'First up need to find somewhere to do our clients laundry before we lose them.'

They get in the Toyota and drive off. Dougal leans into me, and says, 'What are you hiding from us about dis fire?'

'What do you mean?'

'Who started it?'

'No idea.'

'You sure about dat?'

'Yeah.'

'Dis is your grandfather we're talking about. Your own flesh 'n blood. Know something, suspect something, you tell him right away. You owe him dat.'

The manager waves at us and says, 'Goodbye.'

Dalilah skips over to us and says, 'Hi.'

'Hi Dalilah, I'm Dougal, Horatio's cuz.'

'You worked at the launderette right, remember that.'

'Yeah, did a whole summer.'

'What are you two up to now?'

I say, 'We're going to the beach to rent kayaks.'

'Can I come?'

'Yeah come along,' I say. 'We're renting two kayaks.'

'Room for me in yours then.'

I put on my baseball cap and sunglasses. Dalilah grips onto my elbow. We buy two bottles of water from the shack shop, then go to the beach and rent the kayaks. Dalilah goes in the front, me in the rear. We paddle out from the beach, swerve left and paddle towards the headland, which is approximately three quarters of a mile away. Dougal's kayak is ten metres to our right. There is almost no breeze, the sea is calm, and the water is clear. Dalilah says, 'Blissful on the water ... Look!' She is pointing out to sea. Two large birds are flapping above the water. 'Pelicans.' On the right of the kayak, a large silver fish leaps out of the water and lands with a splash. Dalilah shrieks, 'Big fish that.'

'Barracuda!' shouts Dougal. 'Better watch yourself Dalilah, he was looking hungry.'

'They don't eat people them barracudas.'

'They'll have a bite if dey like the look of dem. And he liked de look of you.'

'How do you know it was a he?'

'Could tell.'

She giggles and says, 'No way you could.'

She sticks her paddle in the sea, brings it up in the air, and throws water at Dougal. But he is too far away. He laughs; she tries again. The kayak is teetering from side to side. I say, 'Stop doing that, or we'll capsize.'

An expensive looking speed boat has moored near us. The couple on board are waving. Dalilah waves … We are bobbing up and down by a big boulder underneath the headland. It is a steep cliff, nearly vertical in places, with an overhang jutting over the sea. My paddle is on the left side of the kayak and I am back paddling. We swerve around the headland. Dalilah swivels in her seat – 'Nice steering.'

On the other side of the headland is another sandy beach with a line of luxurious looking holiday homes behind it. Dougal shouts, 'Turtle!'

Between the two kayaks a turtle has raised its head above the water. Dalilah gasps. The turtle's head retracts and it dives under the water. Dalilah swivels around again.

'You see the turtle?'

'Yes, I saw it.'

'Amazing!' She is smiling, showing her pearly white teeth. 'So lucky we are to see a turtle, not often you see them.' We paddle the length of the beach, turn one hundred and eighty degrees, and go back the way we came.

'Race you to the headland.'

'Alright!' shouts Dougal. 'You'll lose though.'

He has a head start on us of five metres or so. Doesn't take many strokes to catch up with him. For every four strokes of my paddle on the right side of the kayak, I do one stroke on the left. This is to keep the kayak on a straight course, as I am paddling harder than Dalilah, and if I didn't we would veer to the left. We are already at the headland. Dougal is at least twenty metres behind us. Too much smoking. Dalilah raises her paddle above her head with both arms.

'We won.'

Dougal is coughing. Yes, too much smoking. Between coughs he says, 'Was outnumbered.'

We are paddling slowly towards the rental place at the far end of the beach. Dougal is quite far ahead of us now. Dalilah says, 'If Javel did start the fire, he's not exactly making your life worse. Rather be here than in the launderette, right?'

'Yes, this is better than the launderette.'

'We had so much fun.' She stops paddling. 'Take it you told your grandfather it could've been Javel?' While I think what to say, I tap the fingertips of my left hand against the side of the kayak. *If she knows I didn't tell him, she will want to know why. I won't be telling him because if Javel did start the fire and the police find out, Javel might tell them I have been buying drugs, and Mum and the others could find out. Don't want that, even if there's no evidence.* 'Didn't hear me. Said did you tell your grandfather that maybe it was Javel who did it? Sort of makes sense. He don't like you and he's jealous. Maybe the pankoot thought the fire was the only way he could get back at you, even though it's not really you he's hurting.'

Will pretend I did. I say, 'Mentioned it to him, yeah. Don't say anything to Dougal though, he has a bad temper and might get angry and try and take revenge on Javel. I don't want that. If Javel started the fire, there has to be proof he did it. And the police will have to deal with him themselves, not Dougal.'

'Won't breathe a word.'

After returning the kayaks, we get ice cream from a food van parked between the beach and the road. I opt for pistachio. There are tables set up in front of the van. We sit at a table. At another table, there is a group of tourists. One of them is the Canadian tourist. She is eyeing me and whispering to the young man next to her. This pistachio tastes good. The tourists come over. The young man the Canadian was talking to says to me, 'Yo, what's up?'

'Not a lot, eating ice cream.'

The Canadian and the other tourists chat with Dalilah and Dougal. Hear Dalilah say to a girl, 'Your necklace is beautiful.' She is fingering it. 'So bright and white.'

Dougal bumps fists with the only other man from the group and tells him about the turtle we saw. Now they are all chatting together apart from the young man who spoke to me. He lowers himself onto the chair next to mine, and says, 'After more of what you got for my friend.'

'Keep your voice down, don't want the others knowing.'

'No probs dude.'

I put my hand in front of my mouth, and say, 'Give me your phone number. Will phone you when I've got it, shouldn't be too long.'

He tells me his number and I input it into my phone which I am holding underneath the table.

'After two G's.'

He walks off and speaks with the Canadian. Dougal says, 'Nice meeting you all. Enjoy your holiday.'

I finish my ice cream and text the dealer. Dalilah is still chatting with the other girls. I go over to her. When I pass the Canadian, she *tuts*. Dalilah says, 'Have a fun time everyone. Bye.' We leave. 'Best get home, my muma needs me.'

I will walk with her and then go on to the dealer. He hasn't texted me yet, but chances are he'll be in. On the road, Dougal stops at the bus stop and says goodbye to Dalilah. They hug. I walk on with her. We cross the road, turn left up the track and walk up to the shanty.

'Was so much fun today especially seeing that turtle.' She stops at the top of the track. 'Say goodbye here.' She throws her arms around my neck and kisses me on the lips. 'Enjoy the rest of your day.'

Dalilah walks off to the right towards her house. She looks over her shoulder and waves at me. When she disappears around a bend, I make my way to the dealer's house. His car is here. I phone him and tell him I'm outside. He stumbles out of the shack, unlatches the gate, and says, 'Enter Redmem.'

As I walk through the front yard the dog growls at me. Inside the shack it's stuffy and there is this rank smell. A crack smoke bio combo. There is a dirty looking young woman in here. She hugs me and says, 'Hi, I'm Francine.' She has a French accent, long lank blonde hair, and stained teeth. 'Nice to meet you. What's your name?'

'Horatio.'

'*Oh!* Famous name, Horatio.' She clicks her fingers. The fingernails have dirt under them. 'Horatio Nelson, that's it. I'm from France, we didn't get on so well with Horatio Nelson.'

'That's right, he gave you lot an ass whooping.'

She does this high-pitched laugh, grips onto the arm of the dealer, and says, 'This kid is *so* funny.'

They collapse onto the shabby sofa and kiss. Full-on, tongues in mouths. Her blonde hair is not silky like Serena's and it's full of split ends. If Serena was seven years older, didn't have designer clothes, didn't go to the expensive dentist her mother takes her to, didn't varnish her nails, didn't have her hair done at the hairdressers, didn't wash and brush it all the time, and was on drugs, this could be her. Poor Man's Serena.

'*Serena du pauvre?*'

She removes her mouth from the drug dealer's mouth, and says, 'Kid, you say something?'

83

'No.'

'Oh, thought you did. Must be wasted. Hihi.'

I text the tourist and tell him to meet me by the food van in twenty minutes. It's a fair walk from here. Poor Man's Serena is snorting a line of cocaine off a broken piece of mirror. She rubs the tip of her nose and clambers off the sofa. The dealer is gripping onto the fabric of her grubby jeans.

'Got to go.' She pulls herself free. '*Au revoir.*'

On the way out of the shack, she pinches my forearm with her dirty fingernails. Poor Man's Serena is a compliment; I'm naming her Destitute Man's Serena.

'Haha …'

'Joke sweet, Redmem.'

'What?'

'What's so funny?'

'Nothing.' The dealer is wiping his sweaty face with his palms. He is in a state, seems kind of agitated. 'I want two grammes.'

He empties cocaine onto electric scales. Through the only window's grimy glass, I see three male youths getting out of a beat-up car. One of them is Javel. His left hand is wrapped in a bandage. That's why the neighbour heard a shriek, the imbecile burnt himself. They go inside Javel's shack. The dealer passes me the drugs, I give him the money and head for the door. When I look over my shoulder, the dealer is standing on tiptoes and reaching up above some shelves at the rear of the room. He pulls down a blue moneybox. So that is where he keeps his drug money. Wonder how much is in there. I open the door, the dog growls at me, and the dealer shouts, 'Dawg'll tear you to pieces, Redmem.'

He stumbles over and accompanies me to the gate. The dog wouldn't do anything to me. These types of dogs feed off fear, and I don't feel fear.

*

Have just got back. Mum is sweeping the courtyard. She stops sweeping and says, 'Was about to phone you. I just saw Dougal. You should have come with him.' *Whatever.* She leans the broom against a wall and puts her fists on her hips. 'Told you already, want to know where you are at all times. You're still a kid, you can't just go where you want when you want. Should have told me your plans.' She takes her fists off her hips. 'Come inside.' We go into the house. 'Are you hungry?'

'Quite.'

'There's bread, peanut butter and watermelon.' Mum gets them from the fridge and puts them on the counter. 'Will cut some watermelon for you.' Mum cuts the watermelon with a kitchen knife. 'Your grandfather tells me you were with a very pretty girl this morning.' She puts a slice of watermelon on a plate. 'Well?' I shrug my shoulders. 'What's her name?'

'Dalilah.'

'Lovely Biblical name that.' She passes me the plate. 'You're turning out to be something of a ladies' man.' *Like my father?* 'I'm pleased that lovely girls like Dalilah and Serena want to spend time with my son. Just be careful though, okay. Girls can be quite forward over here, and you're still young.' She swipes a length of curly brown hair off her forehead. 'For you know, sex. A couple of years away yet, I'm hoping.' She is looking at me. 'You don't want to jump into anything you might regret. Do you understand what I'm saying?'

'Yes.'

'Good.'

'Did women like my father?'

Mum grits her teeth and says, 'Don't know, we weren't together for long. He could certainly turn on the charm when he felt like it, that's for sure.' She strokes my arm. 'Need to speak to you about something. Will let you have your food first. I'll finish clearing up outside.' *My father would have been a magnet for women, no question about that.* Am washing up the plates and the

85

knife I used when Mum comes in. 'Sticky out there!' She wipes her face with kitchen roll, drinks a glass of water, and says, 'Sit down, please.'

I sit on a chair at the table; Mum sits opposite me. She sighs and says, 'Tanice is gravely ill, as you know. A-hh, must be so hard for her being on her own. Shaneeka visits of course and my mother went to see her. But she needs me there. We are so close as you know.' *Get on with it and say you're going back.* Her eyes are fixed on mine. 'Thinking of returning to London to be with her. Which would mean leaving you out here. It wouldn't be for long.' Mum reaches across the table and grips my forearm. 'Would pain me to leave you. Just thinking it might be the only way. You're halfway through term after all. What do you think, in principle?'

She lets go of my arm. I look up at the ceiling. Can remember exactly what Mum's father and Genevieve said last Saturday when I listened in on their conversation. Can repeat what Mum's father said, I just have to substitute some of the words. I lower my head.

'Your mother lives up north and Shaneeka can't take the whole responsibility on herself. She's at college and it's a fair way away from London. You can stay at Tanice's house I suppose and visit her every day at the hospital.'

'Wow!' Mum's eyes open wide. 'You understand my thinking exactly. I'm proud of you' She grips my forearm again. 'Would only be for a short time. If something happens.' She shakes her head rapidly several times. 'Ah, once the situation changes, I'll come back. And if that's not how things work out, you'll come and join me in London. Know it all sounds pretty vague, it's just everything is up in the air at the moment. It's a difficult and sad situation and can't predict how things are going to unfold exactly.' She squeezes my forearm. 'Anyway, nothing's finalised yet. Just wanted to see how you feel about it in principle. You'd continue here as normal for the time being. You've got your grandfather and lots of family here. You'll be busy what with school, cricket, and the launderette when it's up and running again.'

*

16:24 – The following Tuesday – I am on the bus. At school today I did more factorisation, learnt some Spanish, and in English told the class my answer to the question, *How does Charlotte Brontë incorporate elements of the Gothic tradition into Jane Eyre?* I had memorised my answer. The teacher was impressed bigtime and so were my classmates. This evening I have *Jane Eyre* homework. Will also be revising some Spanish grammar for a test on Thursday. Not in the mood for studying now, so I look out the window. It has been raining and the vegetation looks really green. Verdant, that's the word to describe it. There are dark storm clouds overhead. It's going to pour. Tourists coming from the beach are looking up at the sky. Others are running along the side of the road. They obviously want to get inside pronto. There is the man I sold cocaine to on Saturday. He is wearing a black baseball cap with a red basketball on the front. Think that is the Toronto Raptors logo. Saw it on the TV at Dougal's. Someone dumps themselves on the seat next to mine. It's Cornelius. He is grinning as usual.

'Explain this to me, it's making no sense at all.'

He puts an open A4 pad on my lap. It has $5(x-2) - y(2-x)$ written on it. Easy … When I get back, Mum's father and Carlton are in the courtyard. Am about to ask Carlton if I can use the boxing bag at his house for a bit when Mum's father says, 'Want a word with you. Put your things inside and come straight out.' I put my mini rucksack in the house. Mum's not in. I have a glass of water and go out to the courtyard. Mum's father says, 'We'll speak outside.'

We walk up to the Toyota, which is parked a little way up the track. Carlton leans against the side of it and folds his arms across his massive chest. Mum's father says, 'We'll have some privacy here. Don't want Genevieve hearing what I have to say. She wouldn't be happy would she, Carlton?'

'Sure wouldn't.'

Mum's father strokes his beard and says, 'Good news is that policeman caught the person who started the fire. Didn't take him long. No wonder the neighbour reported hearing a shriek.' Carlton chuckles. 'The fool burnt himself. Got lighter fuel on his hand.' *Will just say didn't occur to me it was him.* 'Sought treatment at the hospital. That policeman put one and one together. Lives near the launderette does our fire starter. He's from an underprivileged family, has had some trouble with the law.' He prods me in the chest. 'Seems this youth wasn't too happy with you. The policeman didn't say much, but he gave the impression he thought he was jealous about the girl, Dalilah.'

Carlton mutters, 'That girl could turn a man green.'

'Agreed,' says Mum's father. 'The wrong type of man that is.' He prods me in the chest again. 'Well, what do you have to say for yourself?'

I shrug my shoulders, and say, 'What do you mean?'

Carlton says, 'Why didn't you tell us about this fool?'

'Didn't think it was relevant.' I open my arms. 'If it's the same person I'm thinking of, I've only seen him a few times.'

'So,' says Mum's father, 'you've had no trouble with this youth. Is that what you're saying?'

'Yeah, not really. If it's the same idiot I'm thinking of, he sort of glared at me a few times when I was with Dalilah. Didn't think anything of it. Oh, and he shouted a few insults at me. No big deal.'

Carlton *snorts* and Mum's father strokes his beard. He says, 'Hyacinth,' *launderette's manager,* 'is aware of this youth. She mentioned him to me as a possible suspect. Said he had a run in with you outside the launderette, twice.'

'They were no big deal; he was just shouting some insults at me. Does it to everyone, I think. He was doing it to the manager too.'

'Okay then Horatio, that's all. We'll keep this conversation to ourselves. Your mother has quite enough on her plate as it is. She doesn't need any more stress. Got it?'

'Yes.'

'And in future think.'

SEVEN

A WEEK LATER – I am at after school cricket practice. Have spent time in the nets batting and bowling. Now we are doing fielding practice behind the nets. We are standing in a circle surrounding Garfield, who is hitting balls for us to catch. A boy from the year above throws an under-arm ball. Garfield smacks it and it sails through the air. Cornelius shouts, 'Mine!'

He is holding his hands in tight to his chest. He catches the ball, throws it high up in the air and catches it again. There is a break to drink water. The sun is searing hot this afternoon and it's muggy. Everyone goes to the edge of the field. I take off my hat, wipe my face with a hand towel, have a couple of glugs from a bottle of mineral water, and check my phone. There is a text.

....

Today 15:53

Afternoon, 🏏 going well? So pleased you are 💜 the national sport. Going to be out when you get back. Visiting cousins in Willikies. Won't be late. Just wanted 2 say thank you for being so understanding over me 🛫 home 2be with Tanice. Will miss you so much. 💜 Mum XX

....

90

Mum told me yesterday she is returning to London. She is flying next Sunday. Cornelius shouts from the field, 'Horatio, we're waiting for you. You're running on Caribbean time.'

Some of the boys laugh. I put the phone in my bag, put my cricket hat on and return to my position. The boy from the year above throws the ball underarm and Garfield smashes it with the base of his bat. The ball soars upwards. The boy from the year above shouts, 'MINE!' and positions himself underneath the ball. It goes through his fingers and hits the ground.

'Butterfingers,' says Cornelius.

'Sun was in my eyes.'

Garfield smacks the cricket ball. It spins at waist height through the air. I shuffle to my left, dive with my left arm extended, and catch it one handed. Everyone claps … Cricket practice is over. Cornelius fist bumps me – 'Catch of the day that.'

Garfield tugs off a batting glove, and says, 'Top drawer, best catch I've seen in a while.'

There is another text. It is from that man who I sold drugs to last Saturday; the one I saw from the bus wearing the Raptors baseball cap. He is after two more. What with Mum visiting her cousins, no one will notice if I am a bit late.

*

Javel is on a hammock on his shack's porch smoking ganja. Can smell it on the track. He gets off the hammock, goes into the shack and slams the door shut. The dealer is lying on the grass in his front yard wearing headphones and drinking a can of beer. When I go up to the gate, the dog growls at me. The dealer pulls off the headphones, comes over to the gate, and tilts his chin in the direction of Javel's shack.

'Foolie over dere lit de fire at de launderette on de road. Pankoot burnt himself. Babylon is on his back now. Big trouble.'

The dealer opens the gate; I follow him into his shack. What

91

with Javel being in trouble with the police, he won't be ratting on me for buying drugs. They wouldn't believe him even if he did because he's a criminal, and they didn't find any last time. I ask for two grammes. The dealer dumps himself on his rank sofa and pours cocaine onto electric scales on the table in front of him. At the rear of the room on top of the shelves is the blue moneybox. Can see one end of it from here. Attached to a belt loop on his shorts is a keyring. The key to the moneybox will be on it. How much money does he keep in there …? I want it. He is scraping cocaine with a plastic card into a transparent seal bag. Sticking out from underneath the cushion next to him, is the stock of a gun. Looks like one anyway. Must be a gun, a handgun. I stuff the drugs at the bottom of my mini rucksack. The dealer gives me a pinch of ganja, and says, 'Sinsemilla.'

I leave. Told the Canadian man to meet me by the food van again. Can see him behind it pacing in circles. I pass him the drugs; he gives me the money. Have just put the money in my pocket when I see a police pickup truck pull up on the road and that same policeman get out of it. I go to the other side of the van where the serving window is. Am about to ask the woman in it for a can of Coca-Cola when the policeman comes striding up to me and grips onto my elbow.

'Move!'

We go to the other side of the van. He releases his grip on my elbow, and says, 'What're you doing here?'

'Buying a can of Coca-Cola.'

'Don't get funny with me.' He is pointing at me with his right hand. His left is touching the truncheon on his belt. 'Why are you here? Launderette is shut, so have no reason to be here the way I see it.'

'Stopped off here on the way back from cricket practice. About to buy a drink and go for a walk on the beach.'

'Who was that man you were with?'

'A tourist.'

'Gathered that.'

'He's Canadian, I think.'

'You know him?'

'Met him once before.'

'Where and when?'

'Last Saturday, after clearing up the mess from the fire I went kayaking with my cousin and a friend.'

'I asked you where and when?'

'Getting to that bit.' He grips the truncheon. 'He was with loads of tourists. We spoke to them here when we were having ice-cream after kayaking. That's it.'

His right index finger is wagging at me. He says, 'You might think coming from the UK you are smarter than me. You'd be wrong. I am watching your every move.'

He marches off. I don't think I'm smarter; I know I'm smarter ... It's risky selling drugs to tourists around here with that policeman on my case.

*

I am in a café having breakfast with Mum. She is flying later today. I have a gulp of orange juice and look at the boats in the marina. There are some high-end motorboats and a teak yacht with crew on board rigging sails and scrubbing the deck.

'An idyllic setting.' Mum places her cup of cappuccino on its saucer. 'Will miss it. Especially the weather, and you of course.' She reaches across the table and strokes my arm. I have a bite of pain au chocolat. 'It's unfortunate how things have worked out. It's incredibly difficult having to tug myself away from here. A-hh, but it's the only way.' She wipes her cheek with her sleeve; I have another bite of pain au chocolat. 'You appreciate the Tanice situation is up in the air? We just don't know at this stage exactly what's going to happen.' I nod. A girl with long, silky blonde hair is getting onto one of the motorboats. 'Look at me.' I look across the table at Mum. 'All we can do is hope for the best. A-hh, it's not looking good though.'

Aunt Fatso is going to die. Her days gorging on Maltesers are numbered – 'Ha …'

I put my forearm over my mouth to stop myself laughing. Mum says, 'Why are you covering your mouth?'

'No reason.'

'How is your pain au chocolat?'

'Pretty good. This is the first pain au chocolat I've had in Antigua.'

'My almond croissant is yummy.' The motorboat the blonde woman got on is on the move. She is sitting in the back and her long silky blonde hair is trailing behind her. 'As I said everything is up in the air. Horatio!'

'Yes.'

'Stop looking out to sea. Did you forget, I'm leaving today?' I twist my head around. 'You understand what I'm saying? It's impossible to predict what's going to happen at the moment. I get it's not easy for you not knowing. It's all pretty chaotic. Have I made it clear? Or as clear as it can be?'

'Yeah.'

'Keep working hard at school and in the launderette when it reopens.' She has a sip of cappuccino. 'And be nice to everyone. Our family have been incredibly supportive. It's so kind of your grandfather to let you stay on. Otherwise, I would have had to tear you away from school in the middle of term. And with no school for you to go to.'

Mum glances over her shoulder, leans across the table, and says in a quiet voice, 'Be wary of your cousin Dougal. I know he's smoking ganja.' She points at me. 'Don't want you smoking that stuff. Firstly, you're too young. Secondly, people who smoke it are losers. Well, maybe that's not entirely fair. Adults who do it once in a while is one thing. But it makes kids lazy and stupid. You're a top student and far too special to be ruined by that stuff. Trust me, seen enough of the damage it causes, especially here on the island. You are going places; your cousin Dougal is going nowhere.' She has a sip of cappuccino. 'A-hh, a good example. Brandon's friend.' *Her dead boyfriend.* 'Rollie.' *Rat.* 'Smoked that stuff all the time. Probably thought it was cool. It isn't though. He lives like a bum and has achieved absolutely nothing. As you know because you were there, he got arrested in the cemetery at Brandon's funeral for smoking the stuff.'

The police didn't arrest Rat for smoking ganja; they arrested Rat for the erotic asphyxiation paraphernalia they found in his bag – 'Haha …' I stop the laugh with my forearm. Mum is looking down and nibbling on a fingernail. *I put the erotic asphyxiation paraphernalia in Rat's bag.* 'Ha.'

'Is that the time? We best get going, I still have packing to do.' She pays the bill. On the way to the car, she says, 'Promise you'll be on your best behaviour when I'm gone?'

'I promise.'

Inside the car, she says, 'Not sure what your plans are with that girl who lives near the launderette. But I strongly advise, as I've told you already, to wait until you're older before, you know what. If it comes to it though, make sure you use protection.'

She turns the key in the ignition. Mum means a condom. I am still a virgin. I wonder what sex is like. Similar to wanking I guess, but better.

*

17:05 – I take Mum's suitcase out of the Toyota's boot and wheel it over to the airport terminal building. Behind me, Mum is talking with her father. I wait by the automatic door while Mum hugs him. She says she *prays* Tanice will get better, how grateful she is for him looking after me, and how much she enjoyed spending time with him. Hurry up, the traffic is bad at this time of day. It will take ages to drive back. Mum wraps her arms around my neck.

95

'So sorry to leave you like this ... I love you. Be good and have a great time. I'll miss you. Will phone you tomorrow.'

'Goodbye.'

Mum goes into the terminal building and joins the queue for check-in. I can see her through the glass door. She is waving and so is Mum's father.

'Wave at your mother.'

I wave.

*

Three days later – There is no school as it's half term. I have just arrived at the Sir Vivian Richards Stadium for the Second Test between the West Indies and New Zealand. It was built for the 2007 Cricket World Cup and has a capacity of ten thousand. Seen the stadium from a distance, but never been here before. Mum's father, Carlton and Dougal are here. We are walking up the stand's steps to our seats. Mum's father keeps stopping to say hello to people. He shakes a man's hand, and says, 'Enjoy the match.' To another man he says, 'Let's hope we fare better than the First Test.' And to a woman, 'Good to see you, darling.'

In the stand on my right, I see Garfield. He is waving at me. I raise my right arm. The First Test in Trinidad didn't go well for the West Indies. Watched some of it on TV with Mum's father. The West Indies batted okay, but their bowling was terrible and they ended up getting a drubbing. Here are our seats. I am sitting at the end of the row next to Carlton. Mum's father says, 'Ground must be wet.' It's been pouring the last few days and there are big puddles outside the stadium. 'Don't want a repeat of the 2009 debacle. Horatio, you heard what happened?'

'No.'

'Carlton, fill him in.'

Mum's father is talking with Dougal. Carlton leans his massive frame against the back of his seat, and says, 'Was the test match with England. It was abandoned after only ten balls or so because of the conditions. Same as today, there'd been a lot of rain leading up to the match. Ground staff had laid down extra layers of sand after the rain stopped. It didn't work out so well, as our bowlers couldn't get traction on their run-up. The match was called off.' He lowers his large bald head. 'Big embarrassment it was for West Indies cricket. Made them look like amateurs.'

Dougal is looking this way. He says, 'De media renamed de stadium, Antigua's Three Hundred 'n Sixty-Sixth Beach.'

The West Indies are batting. So far they haven't been taking many risks. Some of the people sitting near me are grumbling about it. I stick my right hand into the pocket of my chinos and feel the three bags of cocaine I brought with me in case anyone is after some. There are tourists here, lots of them. That was two runs. There is applause. Muted is how it would be described … That's a four. Best shot there's been in half an hour or so. The applause is loud. Watching cricket gets boring after a while. It just goes on and on. Unlike basketball, there aren't many breaks. It's a non-stop, steady pace. Need a piss. I leave my seat and go into the stadium's interior. There are lots of people milling about. Some of them are drinking in a bar area.

Inside the toilets, there are three eighteen, nineteen-year-olds boys using the urinals. They are English and posh. Must be from public school. Their parents will be rich. They'll be on holiday, might even have houses out here. They are laughing. Reckon they're drunk. One has blond hair, one has red hair, and the other one is wearing glasses. I take a piss. The boys stumble over to the basin. They are drunk. The one wearing glasses is tall, skinny, and has floppy brown hair. Looks like a young version of that English Conservative politician loads of people want to kill. He says, 'Let's get another beer in.'

'Good call,' says the red-haired boy.

They'll want drugs alright. I approach them and say, 'The West Indies batting is pretty conservative.'

97

'Quite,' says the politician look-alike.

I say, 'But that was a good four just then.'

'We missed that,' says the blond boy. 'We evidently chose the wrong moment to leave our seats.'

'*C'est la vie,*' says the politician look-alike. 'Sure we'll get to see plenty of action yet.'

I say, 'You've been drinking.'

'A few, yes,' says the politician look-alike while washing his hands under the tap. He tilts his head towards the red-haired boy. 'Lightweight he is. Have to watch out for him.'

The red-haired boy laughs, and says, 'You calling me a lightweight?'

'Yes.'

'We'll see about that.'

They are moving towards the exit when I say, 'I've been drinking too, and snorting.'

They spin around. The politician look-alike says, 'You wouldn't by any chance know where to get some?'

'I have some.'

The red-haired boy says, 'Any good?'

'The dogs bollocks.'

'Really,' says the politician look-alike. He strides over to me and adjusts his glasses. 'Do you have any we could buy?'

'Yes, three grammes.'

He looks at the others, and says, 'What do you think boys?'

'I'm in,' says the red-haired boy.

'Me too,' says the blond one.

'Great minds think alike,' says the politician look-alike. 'Very well. Want to try it though; a dab will suffice.'

I pass him one of the bags. He licks the tip of his right middle finger, sticks it into the bag, takes it out, and rubs it across his upper gum. Two men come in and go over to the urinals. The three boys stand with their backs to them. The blond-haired one whispers, 'How is it RuRu?'

'Pretty decent is my first impression. My gum is numb.' The men go over to the basins and wash their hands. When they leave, the politician look-alike says, 'How much do you want for them?'

'A hundred each.'

'Very well.'

He pulls out a wad of cash, counts out the money and passes it to me. I give him the other two bags. Am putting the money in the pocket of my chinos when Carlton walks in. He takes a step towards the urinals. Then he sees me and comes over. The three boys hurry off. Carlton is watching them.

'What did they want?'

'Was just talking to them, they're from England.'

*

07:41 – Saturday – I am on my bed, wrapping an elastic band around a roll of banknotes. Wonder what I'll do with all this money. When I return to London, could buy a smart phone and a PlayStation 5. Problem is Mum would want to know where I got the money from. Could put it towards a car I suppose. A few years from now I'll get my licence. Could invest it in more drugs. Buy in bulk and sell on for profit. Wonder what my father would have done if he were me? I go downstairs, have a glass of orange juice and two pieces of toast with peanut butter. *Ah,* today is my first day back at the launderette. It reopened on Thursday. I can't be arsed to go. Mum is phoning me in five minutes on *WhatsApp.* I go upstairs, brush my teeth, and switch on the iPad. It's ringing.

'Hello.'

'Hi darling, how are you?'

'Fine.'

'School going well?'

'School is okay.'

'Hear they caught the idiot who tried to burn the launderette

99

down.' *Old news, Mum.* 'Teenager your grandfather said. Seventeen. When I was a kid there was almost no crime on the island. Kids had respect. A-hh, Tanice isn't doing great. She has started on a course of chemotherapy. It's hardcore. She's sick and suffering a lot. It's so painful to see.' I am about to yawn, so I move my head away from the screen, as Mum would complain if she saw me do it. 'Feel powerless as there's nothing I can do, other than be there for her. A-hh, praying it all works out …'

While Mum drones on, I think about algebraic fractions. When adding or subtracting algebraic fractions, the first thing to do is to put them onto a common denominator by cross multiplying.

'The doctor told me the chances of the cancer going into remission are remote. A-hh, it's not that I, well any of us, thought the diagnosis was going to be positive. But hearing it from the doctor, it's, ah, heart-breaking …' *When solving equations containing algebraic fractions, the first step is to multiply both sides by a number/expression. This removes the fractions.* 'Horatio.'

'Yes.'

'Remember what I told you about the ganja, don't you?'

'Yes.'

'Good boy … The only positive news is Shaneeka is getting on really well at college. Was so kind of her to come and meet me at the airport …'

After the call, I get my stuff together, put on my trainers, and leave. Mum's father comes out of the other house, and says, 'Good morning. It's your first day back at the launderette. A proper fire door has been installed and a CCTV camera is on the way.' He points at me. 'Listen carefully. You stay well away from that idiot, what's he called?' He clicks his fingers. 'Javel. He's still knocking about. If he knows what's good for him, he won't be going anywhere near my business. And you are not to go up to the neighbourhood above the launderette where he lives. There's no reason for you to be up there. You are to stay well away from there. Understood?'

100

'Yes.'

'Alright. Have a good day then, see you this evening.'

*

Two hours later – I haul a pile of dirty bed linen from the bag it arrived in and carry it over to a washing machine. The sheet by my nose smells salty. The tourist who slept on it is either super sweaty or has been doing a lot of wanking. This job sucks bigtime. I shove the bedding in the washing machine, push it in with my foot, slam the door shut, and wash my hands in the sink. Serena's family wouldn't make her work in a launderette. She'd go psycho if they tried. *Hello, there's no fucking way I'm doing that! Okay.* Detergent, softener, and switch the machine on. There are three more bags of dirty bed linen. *Ahh!* I kick one of the bags then drop my knee on it and unleash punches and elbows, UFC-style. They call this ground and pound. Left hook to the head, right cross to the solar plexus, right elbow to the chin. Goodnight! I move onto the next bag. I push the feet to one side, stand over him and unleash a barrage of straight punches – left, right, left, right, left right. I drop my knee onto his chest and punch – left, right, left.

'What's going on here?' The manager is standing in the entrance to the office. 'Why is it so noisy?'

'Some bags fell over.'

'Hell of a racket they made doing it. Get that dirty linen on; it can't jump into the machines.'

She waddles into the office and closes the door. I stuff rank bed linen in two washing machines, turn them on, wipe my face with a hand towel, look at some Algebra in my maths textbook, then carry a bag of clean tablecloths and napkins to the delivery van that has pulled up in front of the launderette. The driver sticks his arm through the open driver-side window, bumps his fist against mine, and says, 'Good morning.'

'Here's your bag of clean napery.'

'Napery?'

'Napery is a term for tablecloths and napkins.'

'Got it! Place is looking good as new.'

'It has a proper fireproof door.'

'Better late than never. Take it easy.'

He winds up the window and drives off. Found the word *napery* in an online Thesaurus when I was searching for a collective term for table linen. Napery is quicker to say than tablecloths and napkins. It is eleven and time for a break. I will be taking a late lunch today. Dalilah is meeting me now. Here she comes, skipping along the roadside. She is wearing white shorts, a white blouse and white trainers.

'Horatio!'

She throws her arms around my neck and kisses me on the lips. We go to the shack shop. Inside, the woman shopkeeper says, 'What a lovely couple you are.'

I buy two cans of Coca-Cola. We head back the way we came, sipping Coca-Cola as we go. Dalilah says, 'Launderette is looking smart. Your grandfather must be happy it's up and running again. Such a lovely man he is … Haven't seen Javel, thank God. Must be keeping a low profile.'

Dalilah kisses me, says, '*Bye*,' and skips up the track that leads to the shanty. When I enter the launderette, the manager says, 'Such a pretty girl that Dalilah. You are a very lucky boy.'

Luck has nothing to do with it. I move clean bed linen to the drying machines, then press a stack of lime green napkins with a resort's logo on. My phone is ringing. I press the accept call button and hold it to my ear.

'Hello.'

'Yo.' A man. 'You don't know me.'

'So why are you phoning me?'

'I'm Barnabas's buddy.'

'Barnabas?'

'Canadian tourist. Tall, early twenties.'

'Yeah, know him. What do you want?'

'Two of what he got.'

'Okay. Will phone you at five-thirty, be in the area ...'

At lunchtime I buy some fruit, crisps and a chocolate bar from the shack shop then head up to the shanty to buy the drugs for later ... It is smelly and stuffy in the shack. The dealer looks like he just woke up. I give him the money, he counts it, shoves it in a pocket of his shorts, and leaves the room. Wonder if that gun is still under the sofa cushion. I lift the cushion. It's here – a handgun with a black stock and barrel. He's coming. I lower the cushion. The dealer is holding a big see-through bag of white powder. Must be at least twenty grammes in there. He drops onto the sofa and starts untying the bag. Someone outside is shouting in Creole. The dealer mutters, 'Wah you know?' The person is still shouting. 'Empty vessel makes de most noise.' He grunts, gets up off the sofa, crams the bag of cocaine into the left pocket of his shorts, says 'Wait here,' and exits the shack.

I go over to the tiny window at the front of the living room and pull the dirty curtain to one side. The dealer is chatting with an old dreadlocked man wearing a vest. He looks like one of those homeless bums from St. John's. The twenty grammes in that bag sold at full price would earn me two thousand EC. Even if I sold it all in one go to someone at a discount, say sixty, would still be one thousand two hundred. And then there's that blue moneybox on top of the shelves at the rear of the room. I stand on tiptoes. Can see it up there.

They are arguing. Can't hear what they're saying from here. The dealer throws one arm up above his head then pushes the old man in the chest. The old man reels back. He is probably after drugs but doesn't have money, and the dealer doesn't want to give them to him on tick. I let go of the curtain. Could shoot him with the handgun if it has bullets in it, take everything, and leave.

I step over to the sofa, lift the cushion and stroke the handgun's barrel with my fingertips. I pick it up. The clip for the bullets is in the bottom of the stock. Release the clip like so and pull it out. There are bullets in it. The barrel pulls back, that's how to put a bullet in the chamber. And on the side is the safety catch. Push it forward and it's ready to fire. I take two steps back, grip the handgun's stock with both hands and raise it, so that the barrel is aimed at the wall, about sixteen centimetres above the back of the sofa, where the dealer's head would be, if he were sitting here. The body is a bigger and easier target than the head. Could just shoot him in the heart. There's no need though, can't miss from here. Between the eyes is where I will shoot him. *Bang!* Can hear footsteps outside. I put the handgun under the cushion and step away from the sofa. The dealer comes in.

'Wasting my time.'

He collapses onto the sofa directly on top of where the handgun is, tugs the bag of cocaine from his pocket, and empties some onto electric scales on the table in front of him. He gives me the drugs. I leave.

There is a delivery van parked outside the launderette. As usual, it is me who lugs the laundry out of the van, up the steps and into the launderette. The manager never carries anything, she just stays in her office. Might do a bit of pressing occasionally if she feels like it, and that's about it. I drop the last bag of dirty laundry on the floor then wipe my sweaty face and neck with a towel.

The shift has just ended. Fifteen minutes earlier than normal, which is good. Had enough of the place for one day. Was sweating non-stop in there all afternoon. Doing the deal on the beach, as don't want to be dealing near the food van because can be seen from the road. The policeman could be about. I leave the launderette and cross the road. *Beep!* That was a car horn. It is one of the delivery vans. I go to the beach, turn left, and walk along the sand. I am meeting him near the end of the beach.

There are a fair few tourists milling about waiting for the sunset. My customer isn't here though.

Behind the beach are some poles with Caribbean flags hanging from them. In a classroom at school, there is a poster of the Caribbean flags. I have memorised them all. One of the flags on the poles is green and has a cross on it with three bands. The bands are yellow, black and white. In the centre of the flag there is a red circle with stars around it and a parrot in the middle. This is the flag of Dominica. That must be him over there. He said he would be wearing a yellow baseball cap. I approach him, and say, 'Hi.'

'Hello there.'

'Show me the money.'

'Money, what money?'

This man has an English accent. The man on the phone had a Canadian or American accent. I walk off. Another man in a yellow baseball cap has showed up. What are the chances of there being two men wearing yellow baseball caps? The sun is setting and tourists are lined up on the sand taking photographs with their smart phones. When I go over to the man, he says, 'What a sunset, dude.'

'Give me the money.'

He passes me some banknotes. It's all there. I put the drugs in his palm and he slips them into his cargo shorts' pocket. A girl skips up to him, points at a pair of pelicans flying across the sea, and squeals, 'Look, pelicans!'

'Awesome.'

He takes out a smart phone and snaps photos of the pelicans silhouetted against the red sun. The girl says, 'Stunning.'

I am feeling quite hungry, think I will get a hotdog from that food van.

*

The moment I step into the courtyard, Genevieve storms out of the other house.

105

'Where have you been?'

'After work I went for a walk on the beach.'

'You are meant to come straight back here, you know that. You didn't text or phone me or your grandfather to say you'd be late.' *Bossy, she is.* 'Just because your mother is not here, it does not mean you can do whatever you please.'

Mum's father comes out of the house, and says, 'Good evening, Horatio. I hear you were busy today.'

'Certainly was, there were a lot of deliveries.'

He says, 'Come on in.' Genevieve *huffs*. I go into the living room. 'Take a seat.' I sit on the sofa. 'Want a drink?'

'Yes please.'

Can hear him talking with Genevieve in the kitchen. He comes in with a glass of ginger beer with ice in it, passes it to me, sits on a chair opposite me, and says, 'A big relief to have the launderette up and running again.' And now in a quieter voice, 'Don't worry about Genevieve. You weren't too late back, so not the end of the world. But keep us informed in future. And remember what I said about staying away from that neighbourhood.' I have a gulp of ginger beer. 'Girls expect boys to do nice things for them from time to time. You know that, right?'

'Yeah.'

'You should do something nice for that girl, Dalilah.'

'Like what?'

'Take her to a café. The one at the marina you went to with your mother.'

'I could, yeah.'

'You should, she would appreciate it. Now I know you missed out on some earnings what with the launderette being shut.' From a wallet he takes some banknotes. 'Take this.' He passes them to me. 'Put this towards doing something for Dalilah.'

Fifty EC here, about fifteen pounds. Would get two coffees and a pain au chocolat for that in the marina café.

*

08:03 – The following morning – I am still in bed. It would be easy to shoot the dealer and take his money and drugs. Really easy. Only problem would be if people see me. I should do it when it's dark, or when it's quite dark at least. My phone is ringing. It's Bossy. Leave me alone. Will just ignore her. After a while the phone stops ringing.

I stay in bed and think about my first kill, my only kill, Mum's boyfriend Fool's Gold. When I close my eyes, I see him on the sofa in the living room at home in London, dead. His trousers and boxer shorts are around his ankles and his head is drooped forward onto his chest. Can clearly see his bald patch. The belt around his neck is attached by a cord to the metal handle on the window at the rear of the room. On the floor by his feet are two empty beer cans, and on the sofa next to him, a box of tissues and the packet of Viagra I put there. On the coffee table in front of him, his phone is propped up on four DVD boxes – *American Psycho, Casino, Goodfellas,* and *The Texas Chainsaw Massacre.* On the phone, an erotic asphyxiation porn video is playing on a loop. Everything was set up absolutely perfectly. This was the biggest achievement of my life so far. For Fool's Gold, it means an eternity of shame – 'Ha, ha …'

'HORATIO!' *Ahh!* That's Genevieve screaming from the courtyard. *What does she want?* 'HORATIO!'

I get out of bed, go downstairs, open the front door, and stick my head through it – 'What?'

'Good morning is what you say.'

'Good morning.'

'It is time to get ready for church, we are leaving in twenty-five minutes.'

Blrgh! I go upstairs, collapse onto the bed, and put a pillow over my face. The service will be long and incredibly boring. Will be more bearable if I'm stoned. Better get moving. I get up, pull on a T-shirt and shorts, roll a spliff from the ganja the dealer gave me, go to the waste ground below the house, and smoke it. When I enter the courtyard, Genevieve is there. She is wearing a maroon skirt, jacket, and matching hat.

'We are leaving in eight minutes, and you are not even changed!'

Nightmare she is. The police said my father shot that Albanian who shot him at the same time. I wonder if my father killed other people.

*

This church is in Bethesda, a small inland township I have never visited before. Maroon Matriarch comes from here and has family here. The church looks a bit like an English village church. It has a graveyard at the front full of bright flowers. If this church was in *Jane Eyre*, Charlotte Brontë would describe it as quaint. Mum's father and Maroon Matriarch enter the church. I follow them in. They are talking to the vicar. Mum's father says, 'This is my grandson, Horatio.'

The vicar shakes my hand, and says, 'A pleasure to meet you.'

'Likewise.'

I'm lying. He opens his arms and says, 'What do you think of our church?'

'Quaint.'

'Exactly.'

Mum's father and Maroon Matriarch are talking to three old people. They must be the relatives. Maroon Matriarch says, 'Come over here Horatio and meet my cousins.'

There are two men and an ancient woman leaning on a stick. Calling her Cemetery-Bound. Probably the cemetery here. I say *hello* to them. Before coming I put eyedrops in. My eyes are white, so even though I feel super stoned they won't be able to tell. All five sit in a pew near the back of the church. There isn't room for me, so I sit in the pew in front ... The service only started fourteen minutes ago and there have already been two hymns. *Ah, and now there's going to be a third. Annoying all these hymns because it means having to stand up all the time.*

'In Christ alone my hope is found
He is my light, my strength, my song
This cornerstone, this solid ground
Firm through the fiercest drought and storm
What heights of love, what depths of peace
When fears are stilled, when strivings cease
My comforter, my all in all
Here in the love of Christ I stand ...'

Finally, it's over and I can sit down. Sunlight is shining through the stained-glass windows onto me. It is warm and I feel fuzzy. The vicar has just started a sermon.

'One cannot conduct a serious study on the seven deadly sins without first doing an equally serious study on the meaning of sin. The definition of sin is the missing of God's mark ...' *Will be different killing the dealer compared to Fool's Gold because he'll be awake when I kill him. Fool's Gold was passed out from the sleeping pills I put in his beer.* 'Psalms 51:3. For I know my transgressions, and my sin is always before me. God gave man a conscience. When someone sins, they feel guilty ...'

Feeling sleepy with the sun shining on me. The moment I close my eyes, dead Fool's Gold appears in my mind. He's on the sofa with his head drooped forward, a belt around his neck, trousers and boxer shorts around his ankles, a box of tissues and a packet of Viagra on the sofa next to him ... An eternity of shame.

'Ha, ha, ha haha—'

'Silence boy!' Genevieve slaps me on the head. 'How dare you laugh in the House of The Lord.'

The vicar stops talking. Heads turn to face me. If I had the dealer's handgun, I would blow her brains all over her rank maroon outfit.

'Darkness!'

That came from Bossy's pew. Think it was her old cousin, Cemetery-Bound. *Darkness*, what does mean by that?

'Romans 14:23. For whatsoever is not of faith is sin. If you can't do something in full confidence that it is right, it is wrong. Anything that is questionable to you should be avoided like a plague. If you cannot do it with faith that God will bless it, to you it will be sin … I Corinthians 15:56-58. The sting of death is sin, and the strength of sin is the law. But thanks be to God, who gives us the victory through our Lord Jesus Christ. Therefore, my beloved brethren, be steadfast, immovable, always abounding in the work of the Lord, knowing that your labour is not in vain in the Lord. We will now sing,' *Ah!* 'Hymn number thirty-four. *Lo! He Comes with Clouds Descending.*'

'Lo he comes in clouds descending,
Once for helpless sinner slain!
Thousand, thousand saints attending
Swell the triumph of his train:
Hallelujah, Hallelujah, Hallelujah,
All the Angels cry amen …'

Ninety minutes that service was. There's a term for that – overkill. I leave the pew. Bossy and Cemetery-Bound are in the aisle, blocking my exit. Cemetery-Bound prods at me with a withered finger, and screeches, 'Darkness!' Everyone is looking this way. I walk around them and head quickly for the exit. 'DARKNESS!'

She must have senile dementia. I wait by the car. Fifteen minutes later I am still waiting … Here they come. Genevieve is stomping this way. She is in full matriarch mode.

'How dare you laugh in The House of The Lord?'

Mum's father unlocks the car and I get in the back. We drive off. Mum's father says, 'What came over you in there?'

'It has been a long week, have been studying hard, and working at the launderette. It was warm in there and the sun was on my face. Must've fallen asleep and was laughing in my dream.'

'Always have an excuse for your sin, don't you?' She swivels around in her seat. 'But your excuses will not hold up in the Kingdom of Heaven.'

'Darling, that's enough.'

'Did you not listen to the vicar's words. Romans 14:23. For whatsoever is not of faith is sin.'

*

The next day – It is lunchtime, and I am by the school gates eating a packet of salt and vinegar crisps. Lots of boys are out here and it's crowded and noisy. I stuff a handful of crisps into my mouth. These are a starter. Main course is a salami, cheese and lettuce sandwich I made this morning. I unwrap it and take a bite. It tastes pretty good. The salami isn't all that out here, and it is expensive, because it's imported. My phone is vibrating in my trouser pocket. I turn the volume off while I'm at school. It is Dalilah. I swallow the mouthful of sandwich, accept the call, hold the phone to my ear, and cup my hand over my other ear, as otherwise I won't be able to hear.

'Hi Horatio.'

'Hi.'

'How's school?'

'School is alright. Had a Spanish and geography test this morning. Having lunch now outside.'

'There's rain coming, lots of it.'

'Not many clouds in the sky here.'

'They'll be covering the whole island soon enough and Barbuda too. What are you having for lunch?'

'Salt and vinegar crisps, a salami, cheese and lettuce sandwich, and a Snickers.'

'Nice.'

Mum's father said girls expect boys to do nice things for them, and that I should invite Dalilah somewhere. The café at the marina.

'Dalilah.'

'Yes, honey.'

'This Saturday lunchtime, come and have lunch with me at the café at the marina.'

'Ah, so kind of you. Would love to, but helping my muma clean a resort most of Saturday. Might have a spare hour in the afternoon, otherwise will be working flat out all day.'

'Sunday then?'

'Oh, I'd love to. Visiting my grandmother on Sunday though. How about the following Sunday?'

'Sure, I can do next Sunday.'

'Perfect. So looking forward to it.'

EIGHT

SATURDAY MORNING – After cramming a bundle of dirty laundry into a washing machine, I switch it on, and throw two left jabs, followed by a right cross and a left hook to the head. Sweat is trickling down my face. I wipe it off with a hand towel. A mosquito has landed on my left knee. I squash it with my palm. Am about to look at some algebra questions in the maths textbook I brought with me today when there is a knock on the launderette's door. It is a fortyish white woman with long, curly brown hair. She is not carrying laundry.

'Ah, hi there.'

'Hello. What do you want?'

'Um, a tourist I know, an English girl, Emma, came here to do her laundry.' *Skanky Hair.* 'I-is it okay to talk?'

'Yes.' *The manager isn't here.*

'Emma has returned to England. I was speaking to her yesterday on *Facebook* and she mentioned you. She didn't have your phone number unfortunately, so I just turned up hoping you'd be here.' *Get on with it.* 'I'm after you know what. Having a party tonight.'

'How much do you want?'

'Five G's.' *One hundred and fifty EC. Bonanza.* 'You're smiling. Is something amusing you?'

'No.'

'Can you do that for me?'

'Yes, after work. Give me your phone number.'

'Sure. I'm Miriam by the way.' She extends a sinewy, tanned arm and shakes my hand. 'It's zero seven six three …' I enter her number into my phone. 'Will pay on delivery.'

I only have enough money for three on me and don't want to buy on tick, so I tell her, 'Will need the money for two of them. Will front the money for the other three.'

'Ah, well I'd prefer to pay it all on delivery, if you don't mind.'

'Sure, but you'll only be getting three in that case.'

She sighs and says, 'Fine then, how much are they?'

'One hundred each.'

'Um, okay.'

She rummages in a purse with beads on it, pulls out some banknotes and passes them to me. I count them. It's all there. I say, 'Will phone you at five-thirty.'

'Cool. How old are you by the way?'

'Nearly seventeen. Why?'

'No reason, was just wondering.'

I look older than fifteen. The door to the launderette opens. It's the manager. She says, 'Good afternoon, can I help you?'

'Ah, I'm good, thanks.'

The woman leaves. I pull clean laundry from a washing machine and stick it in a drying machine.

'What did that woman want?'

'She wanted to know if she could do her washing here.'

'But she didn't have any laundry with her.'

'She was just asking, enquiring.'

'Why wouldn't she do that by phone? Makes no sense walking all the way here from wherever she is staying in the heat of the day. Tourists, too much time on their hands.' The manager goes into the office. *Maybe I'll get the chance to kill and rob the dealer today. Beeep!* That was a car horn. *It's probably a delivery.* The manager sticks her head out of the office. 'Horatio, delivery!'

I pull the two blue linen bags from the back of the delivery van, drag one up the steps, then go and get the other. After dealing with the dirty laundry, I have a drink of water. There is a heap of tablecloths to press. *Ahh!* I dump myself on a bench and rub my forehead with my knuckles. Carlton strides in. In his thick arms, he is cradling a laptop and wires. He says, 'Good afternoon.'

Afternoon? Yeah, it's 12:07. 'Hello.'

He's here to set up the CCTV camera. It will be connected to that laptop and the computer in the office. Instead of pressing tablecloths, I could install the camera. I'm good on computers, and it would be more interesting than pressing. Carlton goes into the office; I stay sitting on the bench. The manager comes out of the office.

'How are those tablecloths coming along?'

'Getting there.'

'Pile hasn't got any smaller.'

Bossy she is. So many of the women here are. I sigh, get off the bench, tug a tablecloth off the top of the pile, and pull it through the press. Bet I am the only English teenager in Antigua working in a launderette today. Those three posh public-school boys from the test match toilets won't be working in a launderette, that's for sure. They have probably never been in a launderette in their lives. Right now, they'll be at the beach or maybe they have just arrived at a restaurant for lunch. They could be getting on the drugs early and/or cruising on a high-end motorboat, possibly with the young woman with the long, silky blonde hair I saw at the café at the marina when I was with Mum.

Three tablecloths done … Four done … Now for number five. This resort will have the best pressed tablecloths in the whole of Antigua and Barbuda. My phone *beeps*. It is a text from Dalilah. She is cleaning at a resort today, but she plans to drop by the launderette this afternoon during her break. Right, time for lunch. I put on the baseball cap I brought with me, as it's searing hot out there, and don't want the sun shining on my head. I wander down to the shack shop. Want something more filling than crisps and fruit, so I buy two cups of instant noodles, a can of Coca-Cola and a Snickers, and then walk back to the launderette. On the way, I eat the Snickers. Chocolate is pretty expensive over here. This small Snickers costs as much as a Snickers duo from an expensive shop in England, like M&S or Waitrose. Carlton is on a stepladder on the porch, securing a CCTV camera above the entrance with an electric screwdriver. He says, 'Alright?'

'Hi.'

I get the kettle from the office, boil some water, and prepare the instant noodles. A mountain of napkins and aprons have appeared next to the presser. *Fuck!* And Mum told me Antigua was a paradise. Carlton comes into the launderette, brushes his palms together, and says, 'All done.'

The manager comes in, and says, 'Showing up on both computers, clear as day.' She passes him the laptop he came with. 'How's your little one doing?'

'Really well. I took her to the waterpark this morning.' He takes out his phone. 'This is her on the slide.'

'*Arrr*, she's having the time of her life. How sweet.'

Carlton says *goodbye* and leaves. I take a tablecloth from the pile and press it … After pressing the tablecloths, I move clean laundry from the washing machines to the drying machines. Following a jab, jab, right cross, I have a gulp of water and pat my face dry with a hand towel. The manager waddles out of the office and says, 'Popping out for a bit. Will be at least an hour.'

'Fine.'

She inspects the pressed tablecloths, says, 'Good job,' and leaves.

I look at the maths textbook I brought with me, then load a linen bag with the tablecloths ready for collection. Have just finished loading it when Dalilah skips into the launderette. She is wearing a tight pink T-shirt and white shorts. She kisses me on the mouth and says, 'Been working flat out all day. It's nice to have a break and see you. How's your day been?'

'Nightmare. There have been tonnes of dirty laundry.'

'Looking up now though.' She winks at me. 'Where's Hyacinth?'

'Just left. Says she won't be back for at least an hour.'

Dalilah makes an oval shape with her mouth, then says, 'Got the place to ourselves.' She slides her hand under my T-shirt and strokes my back. 'Anything urgent that needs doing?'

'No. There's a collection due in.' I check the time on my Swatch. 'Half an hour. It will probably be late.'

She flaps her hands in front of her face, and says, 'Hot in here. How's it in the office?'

'Much better, there's aircon in there.'

'Think she'd mind if we went in?'

I shrug my shoulders, and say, 'Doubt it. Doesn't matter anyway, she won't know.'

She grasps the fingers of my right hand, pulls me into the office, and perches on the edge of the manager's desk. I pick up the aircon controller, switch the aircon on, and turn it down to twenty degrees. She places both hands under my T-shirt and strokes my stomach. I put the aircon controller on the desk. She pulls her hands out from underneath my T-shirt, places her left hand behind my neck, pulls me to her, puts her tongue in my mouth, and wriggles it about. She removes her mouth from mine, twists her head to the right, and looks at the door.

'Lock it.'

I go over to the door, twist the key in the lock and return to the desk. She pulls my T-shirt over my head then kisses me on the mouth and rubs her hands up and down my sides. I put my hands under her T-shirt and feel her small breasts. She removes her mouth from mine, slides off the desk and slips off her trainers, T-shirt and shorts. Now she is only wearing white ankle length socks, lilac-coloured panties and a bra. She giggles, throws her arms around my neck, jumps up and wraps her legs around my

117

waist. I set her down on the desk. Her tongue is in my mouth again. She undoes the knot on the front of my shorts. They slide down my legs and I step out of them. She grips my cock in her left hand and slides her hand up and down. She makes a cooing noise in my right ear, releases my cock, and lies back on the desk. I pull her panties down her smooth, caramel-coloured legs.

She grabs me around the neck and pushes her tongue into my mouth. I reach behind her and fiddle with her bra strap. It takes a little while to unclasp it. She grips my cock in her right hand and pulls it towards her. So, this is it, I am about to lose my virginity. When I slide my cock inside her she groans, and whispers, 'Don't cum in me.'

I'm pushing in and out quickly now. She is making rasping noises and clinging onto my neck. Can feel the climax starting to come on, so slow down a bit to make it last longer. Then I start pumping hard. The climax is coming on again. One more pump. That's it. I pull my cock out and ejaculate on her stomach. She pecks me on the lips then traces her finger over the spunk. On the other side of the desk there is a box tissues. I take a tissue and wipe the end of my cock with it.

'What about me?'

I drag the box of tissues over to her. She takes some and wipes the spunk off her stomach. We get changed. In the launderette she says, 'How was that for you?'

'Good.'

'Me too.'

We talk for a while, then she leaves. I get my maths textbook from my mini rucksack and sit on the bench. I open the textbook at a random page. *Solve the equation $5x - 12 = 3x + 4$.* Simple … A van is here to collect the tablecloths. It's late. I lug the bag to the van and put it in the back. When the manager returns, I am pulling laundry from one of the drying machines. She says, 'How are you getting on?'

'Fine.'

'Traffic was terrible coming out of St. John's because of the roadworks. Never-ending those roadworks. Endless.'

There is only half an hour until the shift ends. Then I'll go and get those drugs for that tourist. Don't want to text the dealer from my phone just in case I get a chance to kill and rob him. Would be a problem if the authorities checked his phone records and saw I'd phoned him around the time he was shot. Unlikely that would happen, as they are pretty unprofessional over here. But it's possible. Will just pole up; he's usually in.

The shift is over, and not a moment too soon. I make my way up to the shanty. It's starting to get dark. His car is there as always; there is no sign of Javel. When I approach the dealer's gate, his dog growls at me as usual. Not going to text or phone him, and don't want to shout as the neighbours might hear me. The dog is still growling. I open the gate. The dog growls, and that's all it does. I close the gate, walk through the front yard, and knock on the shack's door. The dealer pulls it open.

'Foolie, crass'll eat you alive!'

'Crass?'

'Dawg.' I go inside the shack. It's smoky and stuffy in here. The dealer dumps himself on the sofa. 'What you wanting?'

'Five grammes.'

'Coming up.' He takes a bag of cocaine from under the table, picks at the knot holding it shut, and says, 'Wah gwaan?'

'Not a lot, was working at a launderette all day.'

'Launderette on de road?'

'Yes.'

He is still picking at the knot. He *tuts*, and says, 'Launderette de foolie, me nabor Javel ragged up, lit de fire at?'

'Yes.'

'Pankoot.' Finally, he's undone the knot. 'Moon run fast but day ketch um.'

'What's that mean?'

'Your misdeeds eventually catch up with you.'

119

'Javel?'

'Right.'

He is tipping the bag over the electric scales on the table in front of him when his phone rings. He takes it from the pocket of his shorts, stares at it, says, 'Scunt,' and answers it. 'Monee, ah way eeday?' He stands up and flaps his spare hand, his left hand, about in the air. 'Monee … Nah, nah *nah*. Monee not ride.'

He picks up the bag of cocaine, strides off and goes into another room. Can hear him in there talking in Creole. This is the chance I've been waiting for. I step over to the sofa and lift the cushion. The handgun is here. I pick it up and take the clip out of the bottom of the stock. It's got six brass-cased bullets in it. I pull back the barrel. It's loaded. This is happening. I keep the safety catch on, tuck the handgun in the waistband of my shorts behind my back, step away from the sofa, and lean with my back to the wall. Once he's sitting again will whip it out and shoot him dead. Easy.

He is still talking in the other room. I hear him shout, 'Kiss me rass …!' That was a toilet flushing. Here he comes. He is holding the phone at waist height. 'Rank ride dat warbean.' He dumps himself on the sofa and drops the phone on the table. 'Warbean, slut in Creole.'

Straight between the eyes, then take everything, and when the coast is clear leave. He pulls the bag of cocaine from his shorts' pocket and sprinkles some onto the electric scales. I reach behind me with my right arm and grip the handgun's stock. He lowers his head, drags powder off the scales into a transparent seal bag, and mutters, 'Warbean gave me de claps.'

I remove the handgun from the waistband of my shorts, click off the safety catch, hold it in both hands, extend my arms, raise them, and point it at his bowed, dreadlocked head. He mutters something in Creole and pushes the rest of the cocaine off the scales into the bag. I breathe in slowly. He is lifting his head. His red eyes open wide.

120

'Drop it!' I inhale slowly through my nose and exhale through my mouth. My arms are steady. The end of the barrel is aimed directly at the middle of his forehead. 'Redmem.' He starts rising to his feet, but then lowers himself. Both palms extend towards me. They are trembling. And so is his voice when he speaks. 'E-easy.' My right index finger is pressing on the trigger. He is still holding his palms out. 'Monee, drugs, tek it!' I breathe out slowly. 'N-n-nah.' I take a half breath in and squeeze the trigger. *BANG!* The recoil jolts my shoulder back. 'MAHHH!' He is meant to be dead, not shrieking. 'MAHHH!'

He topples over on his side on the sofa and presses his hands to his head. The top of his left little finger is missing. That's why he's not dead, the bullet hit the finger on the way to his head, and there wasn't enough power in the bullet to do the job. I better finish him off. The dealer flops off the sofa and crawls on his elbows and knees across the floor. That *bang* was pretty loud and I don't want any more of them. With my left hand I pick up a small cushion from the sofa, stand over him, place the cushion on the back of his head, and press the barrel to it.

'*Mee.*'

He sounds like a little girl. I press the trigger. The shot is muffled by the cushion and doesn't make much noise. I fire again. He collapses face first on the filthy floor. When I pull the cushion away, some white fluff billows out of the two holes in it. Blood is oozing from two holes in his head and seeping into his dread-locks. I lower myself onto the sofa and go through in my mind what needs to be done. When I'm finished here will text Mum's father that I will be late back because I went to see the sunset on the beach and missed the bus. I put the cocaine the dealer weighed out for that tourist in the pocket of my shorts.

At the rear of the shack is a tiny kitchen. It has a gas ring with a saucepan on it that smells chemically, noxious. Must have been used for cooking crack, not food. Next to the gas ring is a grimy counter with a packet of baking soda on it, a half-eaten packet of crisps, and a big bag of dry dog food. Will leave some for the dog before I go. If it's hungry it might bark and the neighbours will think something is up. Some rubber kitchen gloves here he didn't use for cleaning. They are presumably for preparing and handling drugs. I put them on, as don't want my fingerprints all over the shack. If some were found in the living room wouldn't be great; but it wouldn't be the end of the world either. Could just say was buying ganja off him, and that's why they're there. I wouldn't be in big trouble for that. They'll be loads of fingerprints from customers in there anyway. If they found my fingerprints in all the rooms though, it would look suspicious. Doubt they'll even be a professional investigation. This is Antigua, and he's just some good-for-nothing drug dealer. How much is in that moneybox?

In the living room, I put my foot on the second shelf, hoist myself up, and take down the moneybox. I remove the keyring attached to the belt loop on the dealer's trousers. This tiny key must be it. It is. Come on, be full of money. I stick the key in, twist it, take a deep breath in through my nose, and open the box. Inside there is a small wad of cash. Disappointing this. I count the money. Two thousand EC, which is roughly six hundred pounds. I pull my money out of the dealer's pocket and add it to the wad. Then I search the property room by room. Other than a smallish bag of high-end looking ganja, there isn't anything of value. Well, there's his smart phone and the necklace and rings he is wearing. However, they could be traced to him and it would be stupid to take them. The shack's bedroom is stuffy, has no windows, and no bed, only a dirty mattress on the floor. The bathroom is minute, rank, and has no bathtub or shower just a toilet missing its seat, a basin with no tap, and a bucket.

I stash the drugs and cash in a plastic bag I find in the kitchen. In the living room, I text the tourist. She texts straight away telling me to meet her at the far end of the beach near where the tourist villas are. The dealer's phone is ringing. Seven, eight seconds after it stops ringing, it starts ringing again. I switch the phone off.

Won't be long until druggies pole up here looking for him. It is dark outside. Time to get going. What do I do with the handgun? Dump it somewhere is the best idea. I remove the remaining bullets from it and chuck them under the sofa then give the handgun a wipe down with a cloth from the kitchen.

I am filling up a plastic bag with dried dog food when it dawns on me what I could do with the handgun. Leave it outside Javel's shack. No doubt the gangster wannabe would take it. And he would be in possession of the murder weapon. I clap my hands. What a brilliant idea. As Javel is a criminal and the dealer's neighbour, the police will probably suspect him anyway. They might even search his shack and find it.

I place the handgun in the bag with the drugs and money, put on my baseball cap, pull the bib down so it is covering most of my face, and then switch off the living room light. The moment I exit the shack, the dog growls. No one is outside and the lights are off in the surrounding shacks, including Javel's. After gently closing the front door, I throw a handful of dog food on the ground. The dog eats it. I sprinkle dog food all over the yard. No one is around and the only noises are croaking tree frogs and reggae music coming from a shack on my right. I jog past the dealer's car and across the track to Javel's shack. After checking the coast is clear, I tiptoe up the creaking steps to his porch, take the handgun from the plastic bag, place it on the hammock, and hurry off.

Outside a shack, two women are chatting and laughing. A car's headlights are shining on me. I bow my head and keep walking. The bag with the drugs and cash in is stashed behind the launderette. The kitchen gloves are chucked in a bin on the roadside. I go to the beach and turn left. The only sound is the waves rippling on the sand.

NINE

1 2:11 – MONDAY – The English teacher says, 'As you all should know by now, irony occurs when a situation turns out the opposite way one might expect it to. Or when words mean the opposite of what they were intended to mean.'

In these hot and humid conditions, it won't take long for the body to start rotting. He probably already smells pretty bad; he didn't smell great to start off with. I can picture him lying face down on the filthy floor with flies buzzing around him – 'Ha, ha ha.'

'Horatio! Care to share what is so amusing with the class?'

'I was laughing about irony in *Jane Eyre*.'

'Which incidence of irony caused you to laugh in my class?'

Everyone is looking at me. Cornelius is grinning and so is Garfield. I go with, 'I was amused by how ironic it is that characters in the novel use religion to chastise others.' *Know Jane Eyre like the back of my hand.* 'Even though they do not abide by religion themselves.'

'Give us an example?'

'When the supervisor of Jane's school, Mr Brocklehurst, asks her if she enjoys Psalms, she says that she finds them uninteresting. He replies, "That proves you have a wicked heart; and you must pray to God to change it: to give you a new and clean one: to take away your heart of stone and give you a heart of flesh."'

Some of the boys clap. The teacher says, 'Well I never, Horatio. Now tell us, why is what Mr Brocklehurst said ironic?'

'Because a real Christian would be kind to a child. But he is judgmental and he tells the other girls at the school to shun her.'

'I'm impressed.'

Memorised all the study notes too, and answers to example exam questions. Mr Brocklehurst was a white male, Victorian version of Genevieve. The class is over; it is lunchtime. It's crowded outside as usual. I stand in the least busy spot by the gates and look out at the cathedral. I have a roll with egg and bacon in it I made last night, two apples, and two packets of crisps. It is well over thirty degrees and the humidity must be seventy percent or thereabouts. Won't be long before he's … putrefying. That's the word.

'Ha haha.'

'Horatio!' That was Cornelius. 'You've gone crazy.'

Ezequiel says, 'None stop laughing for no reason.'

Garfield says, 'Had an excuse for laughing in class but it wasn't funny.'

They are discussing cricket. It's all Garfield ever talks about. I finish the roll and open a packet of crisps. How long will it be until the body is discovered? And how will it be discovered …? By the neighbours because the smell gets so bad it wafts out of the shack, and they know something's up. Or will it be found by desperate customers who brave the dog, break in, and find him dead. Only time will tell. Yesterday, I weighed the cocaine on kitchen scales in the kitchen in the other house. There is fifteen grammes. Ideally, I want to get rid of the lot in one go. Bit dodgy though dealing near the launderette with that policeman snooping around. Could always find customers somewhere else. I can see two tourists on the other side of the road gazing at the cathedral. They look touristy and keen. Doubt they do drugs, not hard drugs anyway.

Lunch is over, and I am in maths. The teacher is writing on the whiteboard. When I close my eyes, I see the dealer pleading with me to put the handgun down. In slow motion the bullet ejects from the barrel, takes off the top of his left little finger and embeds in his forehead. He flops off the sofa and crawls across the floor. I grab a cushion from the sofa, stand over him, place the cushion on the back of his head, and press the barrel to it. He whines; I fire twice.

'Horatio, you're sleeping!'

I open my eyes and say, 'No.'

The teacher points a marker pen at me as if it were a handgun, and asks, 'What is a quadratic sequence?'

'A sequence of numbers in which the second difference between any two consecutive terms is different.'

'Correct.' He writes a sequence on the whiteboard. 'How would you deal with this sequence?'

Easily is how. 'The first difference is calculated by finding the difference between the consecutive terms ...'

Maths is over, and I'm in Geography. We are learning about earthquakes. Basic stuff everyone should know by our age. I look out of the window. Right now, the dealer is lying face first on the floor. The blood that was oozing from the holes in the back of his head will have dried into crusted dark red trails that wind between the bases of his dreadlocks. Flies will be drinking the blood. The old Rasta may well have turned up and is calling for the dealer from outside the front gate. The dog will stop eating dried pellets off the lawn, rush up to the fence, put its front paws up on it and growl. He would be sure the dealer is in because his car is there. The Rasta would become angry and jump up and down, and the dog would bark even louder.

'Stop looking out of the window.' I swivel my head around. 'At which plate margins do you find earthquakes? Conservative and constructive, constructive and destructive, or all three plate margins?'

126

'All three plate margins. Constructive, conservative, and destructive.'

'Yes, you are right.'

I know.

*

As usual on a Saturday I am toiling in the launderette. Between ten and eleven there were three deliveries. Hauling endless big linen bags up the steps in the heat was hard work. Presently, I'm stuffing the bags from the last delivery into washing machines.

'Ahhh!'

Sick of this. I kick and stomp a linen bag. Then I bend over it and deliver UFC-style ground and pound. *Bam, bam, bam bam ...* Super sweaty now. I grab a hand towel and go onto the porch. Wiping the nape of my neck with the towel when I see a woman with messy, dirty blonde hair coming from the direction of the beach. *Ha*, it's Destitute Man's Serena. I go to the rear of the porch and crouch down, so she won't see me. Destitute Man's Serena comes marching straight past and turns right onto the track leading up to the shanty. Must be heading to the dealer's shack. Keen to see what she does and what's going on up there. I haven't been up there since I shot him a week ago. The manager's out, so could quickly go. I get my baseball cap, as won't be recognised with it on from a distance. The manager's car pulls up. *Damn!* She calls through the open window, 'Horatio, come help me carry these things.'

I lug the detergents and softeners she bought at the cash and carry inside. Then I load the machines with dirty laundry and switch them on. It is time for lunch. Will get some food and head up to the shanty. I straighten my baseball cap, go to the shack shop, buy a packet of crisps, a Snickers, a can of Coca-Cola, and two bananas. Fancy a change from apples. En route to the shanty, I eat a banana and drink the Coca-Cola. If the body had been discovered, I surely would have heard about it. There aren't many murders in Antigua, so the news would spread like wildfire. The manager would have heard about it for sure, and so would Dalilah as she lives close by. This means the dealer must still be in there. Will be in some state by now – bloated, stinking, and covered in maggots.

'Ha …'

Coca-Cola sprays from my mouth. A woman carrying shopping bags is staring at me. I keep walking. Can see the dealer's shack up ahead. Two dogs are barking at me from behind a fence on my left. One of the dogs is the dealer's dog. Whoever lives there must have thought it was abandoned and took it in. The dealer's blue Mustang is still there and there is no police tape across the gate, or anything to suggest the place is a crime scene. He's still in there, must be. I go up to his gate and inhale through my nose. Can't smell anything. I could go up to the front door and have a *sniff*. There is surely a rotting smell seeping out. And I could have a peek through the tiny living room window. I don't want to be seen though because it would look suspicious.

While I think what to do, I nibble on a fingernail. There are a fair few people milling about. Don't want to be loitering here, I will return after work when it's getting dark and am less likely to be seen. A beat-up car blaring reggae music is coming towards me. I turn around and walk back to the launderette.

I am folding freshly pressed bed linen and stacking it in a bag, ready for collection. Will be dark in the shack, as I switched off the living room light. When the manager popped out, I went into the office and found a torch. I drop a pile of pillowcases in the bag and then dump myself on the bench. Bodies decompose at different speeds and in different ways depending on the climate. I have watched a fair bit of crime investigation stuff on TV. In dry … arid conditions, bodies become dried out. Desiccated is the word investigators use. In the heat and in water bodies balloon with gas. When I close my eyes, I see the dealer on the shack's living room floor. He has ballooned to twice his original size and there are dark green blotches all over his face.

'Horatio … HORATIO!'

'Yeah.'

'Pick-up has arrived. You didn't hear them *beeping*! Half asleep you are, bad as your cousin Dougal.'

No, that super stoner is in a league of his own … It is five-thirty. The manager locks up, gets in her car and drives off. I stay on the roadside. The sun is starting to set. Can see it on the other side of the trees that run parallel to the beach. A big orange ball. The sun falls beneath the treeline and immediately the light begins to fade. Will still be a little while until it is dark enough to head up there, so I go up to the porch and eat the banana I have left over from lunch.

It's getting dark now, doesn't take long out here. I make my way up the track to the shanty. Some people gathered outside a shack are chatting and laughing. They are thirty plus metres away from the dealer's place, so they won't notice me. Music is coming from a shack and can see lights on in several others. The dealer's dog and the other dog bark at me when I pass by the fence they are behind. As I approach the dealer's front gate, I feel the torch in the left pocket of my shorts.

I am outside his front gate. When I look over my right shoulder, I see a dim light coming from Javel's porch. Three people are on the porch. Not ideal that. They may have already seen me, and they will for sure if I shine the torch. What now …? Wait for them to go inside? I can't be hanging around here for too long as will be noticed. And I'm meant to be on the bus.

'Who goes dere?' *Ahh, they've seen me. Was a male voice, but not Javel's.* Can see a tall figure standing at the front of the porch. 'Who goes dere?'

My plan is ruined. A torchlight is being shined on me. And whoever it is, is coming this way. I move away from the gate and onto the track. They are blocking my route and shining the torch on me. I take out my torch and shine it on them. It's not Javel, it is a tall skinny boy in his late teens. He shouts something in Creole. Someone is running this way. It's that idiot, Javel. He spits, 'White bwoy, wah you doin' in our nabor-hood?'

'Nothing in particular.'

'Fuck you up!'

He won't, I'll just piss on him again. The skinny boy is holding Javel by his arm. A flabby woman hurries over. She looks twenty years older than Javel. Probably his mother. She says to me, 'Wark.'

I say, 'You mean walk. It has an L in it, not an R. And I will. But first I want to ask Javel if he knows what a quadratic sequence is?'

'Fuck dis!' he spits.

'Quadratic sequence.'

'RAHH!' shouts Javel.

He pulls his arm free and races off to his shack. The woman shrieks, 'Away with you, devil bwoy!'

Now the skinny boy is heading towards the shack. Time to leave. As I walk off, I call out, 'A quadratic sequence is a sequence of numbers in which the second difference between any two consecutive terms is …'

Can hear running feet. A torch is being shined on me. I hold up my torch. It's Javel. He is blocking my way. He is holding the torch in his left hand, and in his right the handgun. Excellent, Javel has the murder weapon. I keep shining the torch on him. He raises the handgun and aims it at my forehead.

'KILL YOU!'

'Go ahead, shoot.'

It's not loaded. The skinny boy rushes over to Javel and grabs him around the waist. And here comes the woman. She shrieks, 'NO!' and presses down on the arm holding the gun.

'DIE!'

Javel is just trying to scare me; he must know there are no

bullets in it. I walk off along the track. People are on the shacks' porches. They presumably heard the commotion and came outside to see what's going on. I turn the torch off and keep walking ... I am waiting at the bus stop. Javel can't comprehend any sort of sequence, let alone a quadratic sequence. A handgun poles up outside his shack and the dealer isn't seen for a whole week. He'd know the dealer had disappeared, as he would've seen customers turning up to score. Destitute Man's Serena, the old Rasta, and others too. Which means the dealer wasn't answering his phone. Yet his car is parked there, so the dealer can't have gone anywhere.

The sequence of possibilities, likelihoods even, is that the handgun either belonged to the dealer, or the person who made him disappear, who then dumped it there. Therefore, logic demands that he doesn't want the handgun in his possession with his fingerprints all over it because if the police found it, he would be blamed for the murder, if the dealer was murdered that is, which is a strong possibility at this point. As Javel was recently arrested for a crime and is a neighbour of the dealer, the sequence of events will lead to him being a suspect anyway. Add the handgun, he's the culprit ... Moron.

*

12:19 – The next day – Have just arrived at the marina. I am eleven minutes early. The sun is baking hot and I got pretty sweaty on the walk from the bus stop. In the public toilets, I splash cold water on my face and pat it dry with some paper towels. The café is half full. The table I sat at with Mum the day she left is free. I take that table, as it has a decent view of the marina. There are some expensive looking boats on the water again. I tell the waitress someone else is joining me. She puts two menus on the table and asks me if I am having a nice day.

Thinking about the dead drug dealer when I see Dalilah

skipping along the promenade. She is dressed in all white, as if she were about to play a tennis match at Wimbledon. Polo shirt, short pleated skirt, ankle length socks, trainers. At one of the tables, a late middle-aged white man with a paunch and a Panama hat is ogling her. He licks his lips. Gross. Dalilah skips over to my table.

'Hey.' I stand up. We kiss each other on the cheek and I pull out a chair for her. 'You're such a gentleman.' She sits down. So do I. 'Such a lovely spot this right on the marina. How did you know about this place? You came here before?'

'Yes, for breakfast with my mum the day she flew back to England.'

'Must be missing her. Can't imagine life without my muma. We're together every day.'

I pick up my menu. Mum's father told me you should act like a gentleman if you want girls to like you. Girls like me anyway, so it isn't relevant. But I might as well try some of the things he recommended. Standing up when they arrive, pulling out a chair for them etc. Red snapper with citrus and fennel salad. Nah, not a big fan of fish. Had some red snapper Carlton cooked on a BBQ the other day. It wasn't bad. But could do with some meat. Thinking *cassoulet* – stew of white beans and pork. She is peering at me over the top of her menu.

'What're you thinking?'

'The *cassoulet*.'

'Tasty, I bet. Thinking bou-illa-baisse.'

'*Bouillabaisse*.'

'Yeah, I love seafood.'

I read the description for the *bouillabaisse*. It is a seafood broth containing snapper, scallops, shrimp, Pernod, white wine. The waitress asks if we are ready to order. Dalilah says, 'Think so. Horatio?'

'Yeah, ready.'

'The bouill-abaisse please and a diet coke.

132

'Alright. And for you?'

'Je voudrais le cassoulet, s'il vous plaît.'

'The *cassoulet*.'

'And a Coca-Cola.'

'Coming up.'

The waitress takes the menus and walks off. Dalilah says, 'You speak some French?'

'Not some; a lot.'

'How come?'

'Learnt it at school in England. Studied it in my free time too.'

'You are so well educated. I speak a little Spanish. Was learning at school ... Would love to be at school or college now, and then go on to university to study horticulture ... Couldn't afford to stay on after my CXC's. Did pretty well in them apart from maths ... Can't wait for my meal. Such a treat this. Thank you for inviting me.' She smiles and tilts her head to the side. 'What have you been up to?'

'School, work. The usual.'

'Been to the beach much?'

'No, not much. Been to the beach for a few walks, but not in the water.'

'Went swimming a few times this week. Was keeping an eye out for that turtle, would love to see it again.' A girl is getting onto a motorboat. It's the same motorboat as last time. And it's the same girl with the long, silky blonde hair, just like Serena's. 'What're you looking at?'

'That motorboat over there.'

'What for?'

Dalilah's eyes have narrowed and she isn't smiling for the first time since she got here. I say, 'It's a nice boat.'

Our food arrives. Mine tastes good. It's also quite filling unlike hers. Looks ornate and tasty enough, but there isn't much of it. She says, 'Never mentioned your father to me.' I grip my fork. *What should I say?* 'Where is he?'

133

'He died.'

'I'm so sorry.' She reaches across the table and touches my forearm. I impale a piece of pork on my fork and put it in my mouth. 'Life can be so difficult.' *Mum shouldn't have lied to me about my father. Is she hiding something else from me …? Need to find out more about him. And want to see his death certificate when I return to London.* Dalilah scoops a prawn out of her bowl. 'Haven't seen or heard from mine in years. My parents divorced when I was nine. He's working in the US now. Has a family over there, I'm told. Would love to meet them, my half brothers, sisters …'

Sitting at a table close to mine is a white male tourist in his late teens. He is with a black girl. Antiguan from the sound of her accent. This is no Dalilah. She has buck teeth. If she had long ears and was munching on a carrot, she could be mistaken for a black rabbit.

'Ha.'

'Something funny.'

'No, something stuck in my throat.'

'How's your aunt doing?'

Told her she was ill with cancer. I say, 'Dying from the sound of things. Mum says it's all up in the air.'

'So sorry.' *No need to be; it's all good. Thinking chocolate soufflé for dessert … Chocolate soufflé it is.* When I ask Dalilah what she wants for dessert, she says, 'I can have dessert too? That's so generous of you.'

Sure is. Good thing I flogged a fair bit of cocaine, as this café isn't cheap. Launderette worker wages don't cut it here. This place is for tourists and Antiguans who are getting money from tourists … The chocolate soufflé is top notch. I've only had chocolate soufflé four or five times before and they weren't as good as this. Just finished and am dabbing my lips with a napkin. It's not one of mine. This place must send their napery to a different launderette, or they wash them themselves.

Dalilah has a couple of spoonfuls left of her crème brûlée.

'Delicious this. Thank you so much.' *Beep!* That was her phone. She is staring at it. Her mouth is hanging open. 'Oh my God! It's a text from my friend. She lives by me. There's police and an ambulance parked outside that drug dealer's yard. One who drives the blue Mustang. She's saying he's dead. Murdered.'

I drop my napkin on the table, and say, 'We'll go there and see what's happening.'

'Okay, I'm nearly done.'

I run inside, pay the bill, come back out, and say, 'Let's go!'

'Give me a sec.'

'Now! Or we'll miss what's happening.'

'Calm down.'

She dabs her lips with a napkin and stands up. I cut through the marina. Dalilah is running behind me. I run up to the road, turn right and keep running. It's the hottest part of the day, the sun is shining, there's barely a cloud in the sky, no breeze, and heat is reflecting off the tarmac. Being stuffed full of *cassoulet* and chocolate soufflé isn't helping. Got to get up there. I increase my pace.

'Wait up!'

No, there's no time to waste. Sweat is pouring off me and cars are honking their horns as they drive past. The turning isn't far, can see it up ahead. I pump my legs and arms faster … I scoot around the corner and run up the track. Breathing hard and my heart is pounding. Not far now. I slide on the soles of my shoes, swerve left and keep running. There's a sizeable group of onlookers gathered outside the dealer's front yard. A police pickup truck and an ambulance are parked on the track behind the dealer's blue Mustang. Phew, arrived on time. Having pushed to the front of the group of onlookers, I bend over, put my hands on my knees, and get my breath back.

'H-h-h-h …'

Dalilah rushes over to me. She's panting hard. She asks a fat woman, 'What's happening?'

'Body in dere, dat no good gangster.'

'Oh my.' Dalilah places her palm on my wet shirt. 'My friend was right. There she is!' Dalilah waves her arm in the air. The friend comes over. 'Came up the moment we got your text.' She slaps my back. 'Running like a maniac he was.'

'Bad man's dead inside,' says the friend. 'Neighbours knew somehow.'

The smell must have alerted them – 'Ha.'

Everyone is chattering away to each other in Creole. Can see through the fence that the dealer's front door is closed. I scan the onlookers and Javel's porch. He's not here, and neither are the two scumbags he was with last time. Come on, what's going on? Dalilah tilts into me.

'Us all watching feels wrong.'

No, it feels right. The onlookers are still chattering away. Someone behind me says, 'A rotten sheep infects de whole flock.'

'Dat man,' says a woman, 'was an advantage tekka.'

I ask Dalilah what advantage tekka means? She says, 'A person who takes advantage of someone else.'

A woman on my right says, 'Moon run fast but day ketch um.'

That's what the dealer said about Javel. Means your actions and misdeeds will eventually catch up with you. And they have caught up with him. What is going on in there? Behind me, Dalilah and her friend are talking non-stop to each other. I check the time on my Swatch. Been here twelve minutes, and nothing's happened. Was musty and smelly in that shack when he was alive. It will be stinking now – 'Ha!'

'You say something?'

That was Dalilah. I say, 'No.'

Why haven't they come out yet? What are they doing in there? The sun is shining on me. I wipe my forehead with my forearm. Can hear the dealer's dog barking. Everyone is chattering away. Dalilah is still talking with her friend. Come on … Wonder where Javel is. Could be someplace else, or inside his shack looking out … Through the fence I see the dealer's door opening. Here we go! I rub my palms together. Someone shouts, 'He's coming out!'

Everyone falls silent. A policeman exits the shack and marches over to the front gate. He is wearing a full-face mask and has a cannister attached to his back. Looks as if he's going scuba diving. *Ha*, must smell bad in there. On the way to the gate, he slips the cannister off and removes his mask. It's the same policeman. He opens the gate and shouts, 'Stand back!'

Everyone shuffles backwards. The policeman stumbles to the pickup truck and puts the cannister and mask in the back of it. Then he goes over to the gate and holds it open. He is no more than two metres away from me. He's seen me. Staring right at me he is with bulging eyes. Dalilah nudges me, and whispers in my ear, 'Why's that policeman looking at you like that?'

I mutter, 'No idea.'

He is still staring at me. Two men in bright green hazmat suits and facemasks are coming out of the shack. They are carrying a stretcher with what must be his body on, wrapped in green plastic. The onlookers gasp. Dalilah says, 'Oh my God.'

The pair teeter with the stretcher towards the front gate, which is being held open by the policeman. The person carrying the front of the stretcher stumbles and trips over. The plastic-wrapped bundle slides forward onto the ground. The onlookers gasp.

'HA!'

The plastic has come off. I stand on tiptoes to get a better look. Can see him clearly. His eyes have ballooned out of their sockets and his bloated, dark purple tongue is protruding from his mouth. Maggots are crawling all over his face and squirming from his nostrils. Fair few flies hovering about too. If only I had a smart phone, I could take pictures. There are gasps. Someone shrieks, 'AHHH!'

Another, 'Sweet Jesus!'

That smell is something else. Onlookers are thrusting their noses and mouths beneath their tops. Some are running away.

'BLRGH!'

That was someone on my left spewing on the ground. The body is being rewrapped in plastic. There are more *BLRGHs'*. People are swatting at the flies. I tilt my nose up and *sniff*. Take the smell of rubbish from the garbage trucks out here, which are bad because of the heat. Multiply that by ten. The crowd has retreated, and I am on my own. The body is loaded onto the stretcher, carried through the gate, shoved in the back of the ambulance, and its doors slammed shut. The policeman is behind the pickup truck staring at me. The fun is over; but what fun it was. Hilarious. I walk off. Dalilah is bent over by the corner of someone's fence. She is whimpering and there is a string of drool hanging from her mouth. Her friend is crouched close by, pulling on her hair, and screeching, 'RANK!'

Dalilah is being sick. What a waste of *bouillabaisse* and crème brûlée. She steps away from the fence and wipes her mouth with her sleeve. The friend comes over and strokes her shoulder. People are bunched together in groups. Some of them are walking off along the track. Both girls are looking at me. Dalilah wipes her mouth with her sleeve, and says, 'How could you be so calm with that going on?'

I shrug my shoulders. The friend says, 'All of us were in shock, freaking out bigtime.' Her left index finger extends towards me. 'Except you!'

'Didn't see much,' says Dalilah. 'Covered my eyes. But that stink. B-b-*blrgh*.'

She's being sick again. When Dalilah finishes being sick, she screws her eyes shut, holds her hands up at shoulder height with the palms facing upwards and the fingers splayed out. She shakes her hands about. Again her friend says, 'Rank.'

Dalilah opens her eyes and lowers her hands. She is looking at me, as is the friend. They're probably expecting me to come up with a reason for why the rotting smell wasn't bothering me. I go with, 'Got a bit of a cold. Having the aircon on so much of the time is why. Can't smell that well. Could smell a bad smell, but it wasn't that strong.'

'Lucky you,' says Dalilah.

'Jealous,' says the friend. 'I will never forget that smell as long as I live.'

'Enough!' says Dalilah. 'Don't say nothing more. Was brutal.'

The ambulance is driving slowly along the track with its light flashing. The dispersing people move out of the way for it. The police pickup truck is still parked on the track. A police car is driving towards us. It parks by the pickup truck. A policeman and a policewoman get out, go up to the dealer's front door and stick tape around it. I make my way over to the edge of the dealer's fence and watch them. Dalilah is tugging on my arm. Once they've taped that door, they'll tape the front gate.

The friend places her arm over Dalilah's shoulders. They walk off along the track. I follow. Can hear a vehicle behind me. It is the police pickup truck. Now it's driving alongside me. The windows are tinted, so can't see inside. But I know that policeman is in there. It drives off down the track. Dalilah twists her head and looks at me.

'Was having such a special day. We should never have come. *Hhh*, ruined it!' Her head twists back around. 'Bad person he was. But no one deserves that.'

He did. The friend says, 'God rest his soul.'

At the corner where the track turns right towards the road, Dalilah hugs me around the neck.

'Thank you so much for lunch. Had a wonderful time before all this.'

*

When I enter the courtyard, Mum's father comes out of his house. He is grinning.

'How did it go?'

139

'Went well.'

He claps his hands, and says, 'Excellent. You showed her a good time?'

'Yes.'

'She liked the café?'

'She did. The food is top rate.'

'So I hear.'

Genevieve comes out of the house, and says, 'You better have treated that girl properly.'

'From what I'm hearing he did.' Nosey old bag *huffs* and goes back inside. 'What did you two eat?'

'I had *cassoulet* and chocolate soufflé. She had *bouillabaisse* and crème brûlée.'

He asks me what *cassoulet* and *bouillabaisse* are. Have just finished telling him when the gate opens and Carlton, his daughter and Dougal come into the courtyard. Carlton's daughter races over to Mum's father and hugs his leg.

'What a lovely welcome, little girl.'

Carlton says, 'Alright?'

Dougal tilts his chin upwards, and says, 'Wah gwaan?'

They talk to Mum's father. He tells them about my date with Dalilah. Then he suggests I go to Carlton's with Dougal. Says I should burn some energy on the boxing bag while I'm up there. There is some cloud cover and a light breeze. The perfect time for a workout. I go inside my house and get changed into a T-shirt and shorts. On the walk to Carlton's, Dougal says, 'De old man's been singing your praises. Says you're doing well at school, working hard at de launderette, treating your lady well. Making out you're a good boy now. Have my doubts.'

TEN

THE FOLLOWING AFTERNOON – Computer class is about to begin, and I am sitting in front of a computer, scanning an Antiguan news website. There is an article about the dealer's death. Well, it's just a few lines. This is the first thing that's been put up online about it, other than a couple of comments by people on *Twitter* and *Instagram*. It says that a body was removed from a residence in the Carshalton area yesterday afternoon. And that a large crowd had gathered outside. Doesn't say his name. States that the cause of death is *homicide*. This morning I told some of my classmates about it. Of course, didn't say I did it. Told them how I came to be there, about the rotting body sliding off the stretcher, and the smell. Not sure they believed me. But now I have this evidence.

'Hey guys, check this out!'

Cornelius comes over and says, 'What's up?'

'The dead body I was telling you about.'

'Not that again.'

He is looking over my shoulder. Some of the others come over, including Garfield. He peers at the computer screen, and says, 'Ah, the rotting body you've been going on about non-stop.'

'Yes.'

'Foul. Remind me never to spend my weekends with you.'

Some of the boys laugh. The teacher enters the classroom, and says, 'Settle down and go to your desks, we've got work to do.'

Garfield grips the mouse and closes the news website. We are sharing a computer. Everyone is sharing, as the school doesn't have enough computers for everyone. 'Today's topic is the fundamentals of data representation ...' *Keen to sell all that cocaine. The simplest way is definitely to do it all at once, or if not in a couple of deals. Need to find a suitable tourist, or a group of partygoing tourists. Reprobates.* 'Computers work in binary. All characters, be they letters, punctuation, or digits are stored as binary numbers. All the characters a computer can use are called a character set ...'

Through the window on my left, I see a youngish tourist couple traipsing along the street between the school and the cathedral. They stop to take photographs of the cathedral with their phones. Bet they're commenting on how dilapidated it is. The woman is wearing what looks like from here to be a sequined hippy-style dress. The man is wearing light blue knee length shorts and a pink polo shirt. Standard well-to-do tourists. They are probably sociable partygoers and drug users with rich families who are prepared to pay a fair whack for high-end cocaine, which is what I've got. Reckon there's a reasonable chance they would take the opportunity to buy a load to last them. And for their friends too.

'The two standard character sets in common use are the American Standard Code for Information Interchange (ASCII) and Unicode. In ASCII, each character has its own assigned number ...'

In the right-side pocket of my trousers, my phone vibrates. I slip it out, hold it under the desk and look at the screen. It's a text.

....

Today, Now

After school you are to come straight here. We need to talk. Don't be dawdling. Your Grandfather.

....

Will miss cricket practice. What does he want? Could be that he now knows about the death and has been told I was there when the body was removed. Gossip spreads like wildfire on this small island. He may ask why I didn't mention anything yesterday. No issue there. People don't generally like death. Will just say I didn't tell him, as thought he wouldn't want to hear. So, I stuck to talking about my lunch date. He won't be happy I was up there though when he told me not to go. But that's not the end of the world. Could say Dalilah was keen to take a look, and I didn't want to leave her.

'In ASCII, A is represented by the decimal number sixty-five. B is sixty-six, and so on up to Z. When data is stored or transmitted, its ASCII number is used, not the character itself ... Switch on your computers.'

*

I have just got in from school and am sitting on the sofa in the other house's living room. Mum's father is standing in front of the sofa glaring at me. I can hear someone moving around upstairs. That will be Genevieve.

'Heard what happened yesterday afternoon.' *No surprise.* 'Didn't take long for the news to reach me. Never does. You should know that by now. I am referring to the dead man, God bless his soul.' He folds his arms. 'Big news it is. A criminal investigation is underway. Murdered he was they're saying. And guess what?' I shrug my shoulders. 'You were seen up there acting suspiciously.' He wags his right index finger in front of my face. 'I told you specifically not to go to that neighbourhood.'

'Yes, I know. But Dalilah got a text about it at lunch, and she wanted to go up there to see for her—'

'Don't you be bringing her into it. You expect me to believe that lovely girl wanted to spend her Sunday at a crime scene.'

'She was interested and—'

143

'Enough I said. You drew some unwanted attention to yourself there. The police want to talk to you. A policeman will be coming up here shortly.' *Bet it's that policeman. What does he want?* Mum's father sighs. 'Took some persuading to get him to come and speak to you informally here, and not drag you to the station for questioning.' He *snorts*. 'Wouldn't tell me what he's planning to ask you. Needless to say this is very troubling. It would never have happened if you'd listened to me and stayed away from that neighbourhood.'

I can hear scampering feet on the stairs. Genevieve bursts into the room and screeches, 'Not just any enquiries, murder enquiries!'

'Awful,' says Mum's father. 'I can't believe it.'

'Tell the truth for once, boy!' She slaps me on the head. *Ah! Bossy bitch.* 'For the sake of our Lord.'

'Enough darling, this isn't helping.' He prods my arm. 'Horatio, what were you doing up there?'

'Was trying to tell you. I was with Dalilah in the café and—'

'He didn't ask you what you were doing in the café!' Genevieve's scrawny neck extends towards me. 'What were you doing by the dead man's house, is what your grandfather's asking.'

'Was about to get to that bit.'

'Well go right ahead,' she says. 'What were you doing there?'

'We were having dessert. I had chocolate soufflé, Dalilah crème brûlée—'

'What's a soufflé and a brûlée got to with anything?' She slaps me on the head again. 'You're either out of your mind, or you're trying to bide time so you can think what lies to spew.'

'Genevieve, let him finish.'

Nightmare that old bag is. Could do with a bullet between the eyes. 'We were eating our desserts when Dalilah gets this text from a friend about a body having been found right by where she lives. She was interested to see what was happening, so we went up there. That's it.'

144

'Highly unlikely!' Genevieve shakes her curly grey-haired head. 'Lovely girl she is I'm told.'

'Exactly, darling. Doesn't make no sense a lovely girl cutting short her lunch to go and see a dead man being removed from a house. Makes no sense at all.'

On the coffee table, Mum's father's phone is vibrating. He picks it up and holds it to his ear – 'The boy's here, come on up.' He lowers the phone and groans. 'The policeman is on his way.' He is pointing at me. 'That better be the whole truth what you told us.'

'Doubtful,' says Genevieve. 'There's no smoke without fire.' She stomps off. On the way upstairs, she shouts, 'Nothing but trouble you are. My cousin observed correctly in church. You are darkness; you have no soul.'

A door slams shut. Mum's father folds his arms again. He says, 'Answer the policeman's questions truthfully, whatever they might be. I want this to be the end of it. Big embarrassment this is for us. I make a big effort to be an upstanding member of the community. And you're ruining it! I hope to hell you've been telling us the truth, and that's all there is to it.' He unfolds his arms. 'Your mother would be beside herself if she knew about this.'

The drugs I took from the dealer are in my room. If the policeman searches it, he will find them. Should hide them outside. I stand up.

'Sit!'

I sit down. He stares at me for a while then lowers himself onto an armchair. Doesn't say much else other than how disappointed he is and how he is at a loss as to why the police want to speak to me. There is no way the police know I killed the dealer. That policeman is probably just suspicious because he suspects I have been selling the dealer's drugs. And he will be wondering how I came to be up there yesterday. Will just stick with my story. Those drugs should be moved though, and quickly. I stand up.

145

'Sit, I said.'

'Just want to sort my things out in the other house.'

'No, you stay put.'

Ah! Seven or eight minutes have passed when Genevieve shouts from upstairs, 'He's arrived!'

I follow Mum's father into the courtyard. He opens the gate. Normally cars park outside on the track. He doesn't want the neighbours knowing the police are here. A police pickup truck drives into the courtyard and Mum's father closes the gate. The policeman gets out, and says, 'I want to talk to him in private.'

'Understood.' Mum's father points at the house where I'm staying. 'You two can talk in there. Let me know when you're done.'

'Will do, Bevis.'

Mum's father walks off to the other house. The policeman is eyeballing me; he doesn't say anything. We go inside. I nudge the front door shut with my foot and take a seat at the table. He sits on the opposite side of the table to me, removes his baseball cap, and places it on the table. He still hasn't said anything. The police questioning someone in their house surely wouldn't happen in the UK. It wouldn't be allowed. Anything goes over here. The policeman puts his elbows on the table and presses the fingertips of both hands together.

'How come you happened to be there yesterday when the body was being removed from the house?'

Will just repeat what I told Genevieve and Mum's father. I say, 'Was at the café at the marina having lunch with my girlfriend.'

'Dalilah?'

'Yes.'

'We were having dessert when she got this text from a friend saying a body had been found right by where she lives. She was interested to see what was happening, so we went up there. That's it.'

'All her idea, was it?'

146

'Yes. And I went along with it. So what?'

He takes out a notebook and writes in it. He puts the notebook and pen on the table, and says, 'You were having a good time; you were acting like you were at a BBQ.' His small, sunken eyes are fixed on my face. 'What do you have to say for yourself?'

'I was acting normally.'

'Nothing normal about it. No one could stand the smell. Retching, vomiting they were. But not you.'

'Had a cold and couldn't smell properly. I got it from the aircon.'

'Be telling me you had an eye infection next and couldn't see anything. You couldn't get enough of that body when it came off the stretcher. Revolting.' *That is not a crime.* 'Transfixed you were.' *Was just looking.* He slides his elbows off the table. 'Didn't show no sign of shock. Not one iota.' He flicks through his notebook, stops at a page, and looks at it. 'Strange thing that.' He closes the notebook and fixes his sunken eyes on me again. They never seem to blink. 'You two knew each other; you were seen at his yard several times.' He places his elbows on the table and presses the fingertips of both hands together. 'Buddies, were you?' *No point in lying as he knows I knew him.* 'Answer me?'

'Knew that man, yeah. He was an acquaintance, that's all.'

'What do you mean by acquaintance exactly? And how did you come to be acquainted?'

Will just say he tried to push me drugs. 'He would drive past the launderette in his car sometimes. A few times I was outside and he spoke to me. And once when I was walking to the shop.'

'What did he want?'

'Always asked if I wanted ganja.'

'And what did you say?'

'I said no, don't smoke the stuff.'

He lifts his eyebrows, and says, 'If you didn't want the ganja he was pushing, what were you doing in his yard?'

While thinking what to say, I tap my fingertips against my

knees. Just tell him he was interested in me because I was foreign.
'He wanted to know all about England. Guessing he didn't get to speak to many foreigners apart from some tourists. He invited me to his a few times. Didn't want to go because he was selling ganja. I don't want to be involved with that sort of person, who does illegal stuff. But I also didn't want to annoy him because thought he might be dangerous, and he knew where I worked.'

'And you expect me to believe this rubbish?' He leans back in the chair. 'You weren't up to any mischief, is that what you're saying?'

'Exactly.'

'You weren't buying drugs off him?'

'No.'

'Sure about that?'

'Yes.'

'You behaved like a saint, did you? Just talking about England and not buying or taking no drugs.'

'Precisely.'

He is peering up at the ceiling. The drugs are upstairs. He looks me in the eyes, and asks, 'You weren't even smoking ganja?' I shrug my shoulders. *It is decriminalised here, so no need to lie. If he thinks I did, it doesn't matter. Not admitting to it though as I don't want Mum's father and Genevieve finding out.* He puts his elbows on the table. 'Where were you on the day he died?' *Like I would fall for that.* 'Why're you smiling? Answer me!'

'That depends.'

'On what?'

'When he died.' The policeman doesn't say anything, he just glares at me with his sunken, unblinking eyes. 'I know it wasn't yesterday; he'd been dead a while.'

'Stop smiling. There's nothing funny about it.' He rubs his chin. 'Moving on. You seen much of that boy of late? The one who started the fire at the launderette. Javel.'

'No, not much. Seen him wandering about a few times, that's it.'

148

'Where?'

'Near the launderette, and one time by the dead ganja dealer's house.' He is writing in the notebook. 'Is this normal procedure?'

He stops writing, and says, 'What do you mean normal procedure?'

'The police turning up at people's houses to question them. In the UK, the police do things officially. They question people in police stations.'

'We can go to the station.' He closes the notebook and puts the pen on the table. 'If that's what you want.'

'I was just saying.'

'Don't you be telling me how we should do things over here. This is not a British colony anymore. Hasn't been since nineteen eighty-one. We do what works for us. Got it?'

He is peering up at the ceiling again. Better not be wondering if there are drugs up there. Wouldn't be good if he searched my room, or brought a sniffer dog. He asks some more questions. Then he says, 'That's it for now.'

The policeman gets up and leaves. Through the window I watch him cross the courtyard and go into the other house. Six minutes have elapsed when he comes out with Mum's father and Genevieve. Mum's father opens the gate, and the policeman drives off. He has no reason to think I killed the dealer and no evidence that I did. There is nothing to worry about; he is no Hercule Poirot. Javel is the main suspect. The policeman asked about him after all. Regardless, I need to find somewhere to hide those drugs just in case he comes back to do a search. Am thinking where I could stash them when Genevieve screams from the courtyard, 'Horatio!'

'Yes.'

'Get over here, right away!'

Bossy as Aunt Fatso she is. I go to the other house. They are sitting on the sofa in the living room. I stand on the rug in front of them. Mum's father says, 'Had a quick word with the policeman. He says that's it for now.'

Genevieve *tuts*. I say, 'Yeah. That policeman must be speaking to everyone who was there yesterday. He's trying to find out what happened, if anyone knows anything. That's it.'

Genevieve *tuts* again and Mum's father says, 'We were thinking along the same lines. Doesn't change the fact you shouldn't have been there in the first place. If you did what I told you to, the police wouldn't be questioning you.' He is wagging his right index finger at me. 'I don't want the police showing up here. Big embarrassment it is. How do you think it makes me look?'

I don't say anything. Genevieve extends her scrawny neck towards me, and says, 'Non-plussed you are. Looks as if you've been reading a book, having a snooze, and not being questioned by the police.'

'I haven't done anything wrong, so I should appear nonplussed. It's a sign of my innocence.'

Genevieve says, 'There's no smoke without fire.'

Mum's father says, 'Any investigation starts off with the police speaking to everyone.' He wags his finger at me again. 'Shouldn't have been there though, should you? You stay away from that neighbourhood. And don't be mentioning this to anyone. It's not in your interests and not in ours that the police have been snooping around.'

*

The next day – School has finished and I am on the bus to cricket practice. Garfield is sitting next to me. In the row in front, Cornelius and another boy are kneeling on their seats and looking over the backs of them. Garfield says, 'What did that policeman want to know?'

'Everything, basically. Why I was there, what I knew.'

Cornelius says, 'Keep your voice down, there are other people on the bus.'

So what? The boy next to Cornelius says, 'Are you saying that

150

policeman thought you were involved in the death? Maybe even killed the man.'

'Put it this way, he tried to trap me.'

'How did he do that?' says Garfield.

'Asked me where I was the day he died.'

'Crafty,' says the other boy. 'Trying to incriminate you.'

Cornelius says, 'How did you answer?'

'Said I didn't know which day he died. The body was rotting—'

'Don't start on that rotting business,' says Garfield. He scrunches up his face. 'Makes me feel queasy.'

'Never smelt a rotting dead body,' says the other boy. 'Let alone seen one.'

'Me neither,' says Cornelius. 'Planning to keep it that way.'

This is our stop. I pick up my bag and get off the bus. Boys gather around me and ask questions. One says, 'Your family must be stressing out bigtime.'

Another says, 'My family would be in turmoil if police showed up at mine questioning me about a murder.'

Cornelius says, 'Any idea who killed that man?'

'There is a suspect in the case.'

'Yeah, you,' says Garfield.

He laughs, as do the others. I say, 'The dealer's neighbour is the likely culprit.'

A boy says, 'Sherlock Holmes has come from England to solve the case.'

There is more laughter. Someone says, 'Who is Sherlock Holmes?'

Garfield says, 'A fictional detective from back in the day. Victorian times. Horatio, who is this neighbour?'

'A moron, a wannabe gangster who lives opposite the dealer. Have a feeling it was him.'

Cornelius says, 'Sticking out like a sore thumb, is he?'

We have arrived at the training ground. Some of the boys put on pads, take cricket bats, and go into the nets. I'm going to be bowling for Garfield, the best batsman in my year, and probably the whole school. While I wait for my turn to bowl, I rub the ball against my top. A boy bowls a ball for Garfield. It never reaches him though as it goes into the side netting. Garfield tells him off. The boy blames it on the sun shining in his eyes. I put on my sunglasses, run up, and bowl. The ball spins through the air and Garfield takes a step forward with his bat held straight out in front of him. The ball comes off the bat and trickles halfway back to me. Good delivery that was, it forced him on the defensive. He wouldn't have got a run off that shot.

*

That evening – I am in my room, studying Spanish grammar for a test at school. The drugs have been put in a plastic box and buried on the waste ground next to the house. If that policeman returns to search the house, he will be embarrassed again. It is nearly seven. Time for some dinner. There isn't much in the fridge or cupboards. Will just have noodles, salad, and a Snickers. While eating, I will watch something on the iPad. *Ah*, but it's in the other house. The bossy cow took it first thing this morning, so her granddaughter could watch cartoons when she came over today. She hasn't returned it. If you borrow something off someone, it should be returned without the other person having to ask. Genevieve is so busy telling everyone else what to do, she has forgotten about her own behaviour. I am approaching the other house when I hear Mum's father talking in the living room. It sounds like he's on the phone. He could be talking to that policeman. I press my back to the wall and slide along it to the mosquito screen-covered living room window.

'Agreed, not good news. Not a surprise though, we suspected it was coming … We'll keep praying.' *It's not the policeman.* 'Spoke to her last night. She tried to sound upbeat, but must be going through hell the poor girl … Such an independent person she is.

152

Must be so difficult being stuck in hospital all day.' *Aunt Fatso.* 'You being there is a big support for her.' *Mum.* 'Got that loud and clear. We haven't said a word to him.' *What is he talking about?* 'Not in the mood today, I quite understand. Got enough on your plate as it is. Tell him later in the week ... He's doing alright. Doing well at school from the sound of things, working at the launderette, playing cricket ... Will do. Love you. Bye for now.'

What does Mum want to talk to me about? I am sliding along the wall when I hear Genevieve say, 'Didn't tell her about the police then.'

'Of course not. My daughter would be distraught if she knew. Regardless, there's no evidence the boy did much wrong, other than being somewhere he shouldn't have been.'

'There is no smoke without fire.'

'Getting tired of that saying.'

Me too.

'Big relief it's coming to an end.'

'Right, I'm off to Dougal's to see if I can fix that brush cutter. His yard is turning into a jungle.'

I walk backwards away from the house. Mum's father opens the front door.

'Oh, evening Horatio. How was your day?'

'Not too bad. Just come to get the iPad.'

*

14:37 – Thursday – I am in English, the last class of the day. While looking out of the window, I think about my stash of cocaine. Moving it to the launderette would be a good idea. There are plenty of hiding places there. Will be easy then to sell it to local tourists when I get a chance.

'Horatio, stop looking out the window!' I twist my head around. 'Tell us, do you think *Jane Eyre* can be considered Gothic?'

'To an extent, yes. There are elements in *Jane Eyre* that are typical of Gothic literature. Take the mysterious buildings for example. In particular Thornwood Manor …'

As always the teacher is impressed by my knowledge. Now he is talking about gender roles in the novel. My phone number has been passed about. However, no one has contacted me since I robbed and killed the dealer. Someone surely will soon. When the time comes, I will push them to take all of it, or at least a lot of it. The teacher is still droning on about gender roles. My phone vibrates. It could be a customer. I slip it out of my pocket and look at the screen underneath the desk. It's a text.

....

Today, Now

Hi Sweetie, Got big news ☺. News sure travels fast!! Fancy meeting up after school? Dalilah xx 🍃 💚

....

We will meet at that food van by the beach. I text her. Wonder what the news could be. Have the police arrested someone? The teacher says, 'Social class is an important theme. Give me an example, Garfield?'

'The complex social position of governesses.'

'Correct. You've finally put your cricket bat away and done some studying.'

*

15:47 – I am walking from the bus stop to the rendezvous point. At a table in front of the food van, I can see a young man wearing a red baseball cap and a woman with dirty blonde hair. Could be

154

that Canadian tourist and Destitute Man's Serena ... It's not them. Dalilah is skipping towards me. She throws her arms around my neck and kisses me on the lips.

'Hey, how are you?'

'Fine.' I buy two cans of Coca-Cola from the food van. We wander down to the beach and drink them there. 'What's the big news?'

'First thing this morning I'm told, the police came and took Javel away.' *Perfect.* I clench my fist. 'Seems he did it. That's what everyone's saying anyway.'

'No surprise there.'

We sit underneath a tree overlooking the sea. Dalilah has a sip from her can of Coca-Cola, and then says, 'Kicking and screaming he was, according to the neighbours who saw him.'

Typical. Was probably pissing himself as well – 'Ha, ha ...'

'Not funny, any of it. Someone was killed and now someone might be spending a large portion of their life behind bars. A tragedy that could have been avoided.'

I prefer a comedy that couldn't have been avoided – 'Ha.'

'Not funny I said.'

She slaps my arm. I say, 'Javel must have been the prime suspect. He's a known criminal who lives opposite the dead dealer. Even the police aren't stupid enough to not put one and one together and suspect it could well be him.'

'People are saying the police have evidence.'

'What evidence?'

She rests her hand on my forearm, and says, 'Neighbours have seen that idiot Javel, drunk, stoned, and waving a gun around. May well have reached the ears of the police.'

'Will be the same handgun he shot the dealer with.'

'Never said it was a handgun.'

'Well, it isn't likely to be a machine gun.'

'Not sure what sort of gun it is. Just hear it was a gun and the police have taken him away.'

She drapes her arm over my shoulders, nibbles my neck, and rubs the inside of my thigh. We have a walk on the beach. Then we go to the bus stop. Dalilah waits with me until my bus arrives, and waves to me as it drives away. Fantastic, the police must have found the handgun at Javel's, and forensics will discover it is the weapon that shot the dealer. If they even have forensics here. Maybe the police get help from somewhere else with forensics. Regardless, case closed. That policeman won't be questioning me again. And Genevieve can't blame me for anything. Javel's arrest proves I'm innocent. Well, when he's convicted it will. And that's only a matter of time.

There doesn't seem to be anyone around and I cross the courtyard without being yelled at by Genevieve for being late back. I have a glass of water, go upstairs to my room and switch on the iPad. Talking to Serena on *WhatsApp* in fifteen minutes. I check the news. There is no mention on any of the Antiguan news sites about the arrest. No surprise there, as doubt there are any professional media outlets here. There is a tweet on *Twitter* though from someone claiming their neighbour has been taken away by the police and they think it's for murder. They think right … Serena is ringing.

'Hello.'

'Hi gorgeous, where are you …?' I switch the video on. 'There you are, can see you now.' Serena's hair is as long, silky looking and blonde as ever. 'What's up?'

'Been at school all day.'

'Don't mention school, it's so boring. I fell asleep twice today in class. How's Antigua?'

'Pretty good.'

'Are there lots of hot girls there?' Serena pouts and tilts her head to the side. 'Tell me?'

'No, only a few.'

'*Okay*, if you say so. I heard there were loads. That's what my friend told me anyway. Oh, that reminds me. I want to ask you

156

about this place she's been telling me about in Antigua. There's this luxury resort on a cliff overlooking the sea. It's called something rocks, think she said.'

'Sheer Rocks.'

'Yeah, might be. Have you been?'

'No.'

'She went diving too with stingrays. Sounded awesome. Have you done that?'

'No, I haven't.'

'Haven't even seen the stingrays.' She sighs. 'Have you seen anything out there at all? And don't say launderette.'

'Saw a dead body.'

'Oh my God. Human?'

'A man.'

'Another one!' She presses her hands to her cheeks. 'What is it with you and dead bodies? Most people have never even seen one, and you've seen two now. And the last one wasn't that long ago. Your mum's boyfriend. You told me all about it. Was this one a traffic accident?'

'No. He was a drug dealer. He died in his house. Was murdered. Been in there a while and was rotting. He smelled terrible.'

Serena fans her fingers in front of her face – 'Gross!'

'Sure was.'

'Not sure I even believe you. I mean how come you saw it?'

'News spreads fast over here, as it's a small island. Heard the police were there, at the dealer's house. Was nearby so I went to see. There was a crowd of onlookers ... The body fell off the stretcher and came uncovered. Was covered in maggots.'

'Grossest thing *ever*. I don't want to know. Just ate like an hour or two ago. It's way grosser than your mum's dead boyfriend. At least he wasn't rotting.' My phone is ringing on the bedside table. It's Mum. *I'm busy, she can phone back later.* 'School sucks as always ... Having tennis coaching once a week and swimming quite a bit. Oh yeah, went shopping last weekend. Got this Dolce

& Gabbana belt. Wait there.' Serena disappears. Mum is phoning again. *What does she want?* 'Like it?' Serena is holding up a shiny black belt with a large silver D and G on the front of it. 'Won't tell you how much it cost. It was a lot. Took ages to persuade Mum to buy it for me ...' My phone is ringing yet again. It's Genevieve's number. I ignore it. 'Going to Singapore soon to see my father. Remember I told you he lives out there.'

'Yes.'

'Been there before. It's quite boring actually. Super clean though and I love the food. They have this giant aquarium. It's awesome ... He lives there with his old secretary. They're married and they've had a kid, a boy. He's a week old. So, I have a brother now! It's a strange feeling, as always been an only child. Sort of cool though. Can't wait to see him. Looks so cute and ...'

'HORATIO!'

Genevieve. *Ahh!* She is calling me from the courtyard. *Go away!* I say to Serena, 'Bossy step-grandmother is calling me.'

'Another bossy relation. Your aunt is super bossy, know that.'

'This one isn't as fat, but just as bossy. Won't be a sec.'

'HORATIO!' I go downstairs and open the front door. 'Why aren't you answering your phone?'

'Because I am on a *WhatsApp* call.'

'Your mother's been trying to get through to you. Wants to speak to you right away. She's going to phone you again in a minute, make sure you pick up.'

I go up to my room. Serena is standing up, wearing the belt. She says, 'Stylish, huh?'

'Sure is.'

'Mum is pissed off my father had a baby. She always hated my step mum cos my father was having an affair with her when they were still married. Still calls her 'The Secretary'. Kind of spits it out like it's a swear word. Good thing Mum is separated from her by seven time zones ...'

My phone is ringing. It is Mum. I say, 'My mum's phoning, got to go.'

'Lovely talking to you. Apart from the bit about the rotting body that is. *Bye.*'

What does Mum need to speak to me about right away? I accept the call and say, 'Hello.'

'How're you doing?'

Her voice sounds sort of weak. I say, 'Fine.'

'How's school?'

'It's okay. Know *Jane Eyre* like the back of my hand now. And got full marks in a Spanish test.'

'Well done. Pleased to hear you're keeping your nose to the grindstone … Wish I had positive news, I really do.' *Sniff.* 'Tanice is not doing well, and, *hhh*, she's not going to be recovering it seems. There's nothing that can be done.' I yawn. 'The cancer is too far gone.'

'How long she got?'

'Just don't know, that's the thing. A-hh, can't tell for sure. Doctor said could be as little as a few months. Six, seven max.' *So, the cancer is going to kill her.* 'Absolutely heart-breaking having to watch your sister go through this … Shaneeka has been so supportive. She's staying here for a few days.' I yawn again. 'She'd love a word when I'm done … Horatio, you there?'

'Yes, I'm here.'

'A-hh, this is the situation then. I won't be returning to Antigua now as need to be with Tanice. And, ah, we just don't know how things are going to pan out timewise. Do you understand?'

'Yes. Aunt Tanice is dying of cancer and you're going to stay in London.'

'Yeah, that's the gist of it. A-hh, the plan is once term is over, you'll return to London.'

'Term ends in just over a week.'

'Know that! Get it's not ideal but our plans went up in smoke. Thought we'd be in Antigua for a year or so. Otherwise, wouldn't

159

have gone through all the hassle of moving there. I'm sorry it's come to this. You've only just settled in there, and it's time to leave … It's the only way though. Can't leave you out there if I'm not there.'

'What about school?'

'I'm looking into that.'

'And our house is rented out.'

'We'll stay at Tanice's flat until the tenants move out of ours …'

Mum keeps talking for ages. At the end of the call, I sit on the bed and peer up at the whirling ceiling fan. I am returning to London. Which means bad weather, not having a house to myself, and a new school. Probably a crap one. On the plus side there'll be no launderette, no mosquitos, and no Genevieve. So, that is what Mum's father and Genevieve were talking about.

ELEVEN

SATURDAY MORNING – I've just had a shower and am drying myself with a towel. Last night there was a family dinner at the other house. It went on for quite a long time. They all know I'm leaving. I lie on the bed, switch on the iPad, and check the Antiguan news websites. Finally, there is something substantial about it. An article on the website *Antigua Newsroom*. I read it. *Eighteen-year-old Carshalton resident Javel Coleridge was arrested at his house on Thursday morning, on suspicion of the murder of a suspected drug dealer … He is currently being held at Her Majesty's Prison in St. John's. A police spokesperson said more details will be revealed in due course.* There is not much information then. The police must have found the handgun. Javel is looking at a decade or two in prison. What an idiot he was keeping hold of it.

Last night in my dreams, I saw the bodies of the two men I've killed. The dealer was just as I left him – planted face first on the floor of the filthy living room with blood oozing from the two holes in his head. Mum's dead boyfriend, Fool's Gold, was on the sofa in the living room in my house in London with a belt around his neck and EA porn playing on his phone.

At the launderette today. I get changed, have a quick breakfast, and brush my teeth. There is a knock on the door. It's Mum's father.

'Good morning, Horatio.'

'Good morning.'

'I'm driving you this morning.'

In the car he says, 'Police have caught the person they think committed the murder.' He swivels his head and looks at me. 'Know who it is?'

'The idiot who tried to burn the launderette down. Javel.'

'You heard the news?'

'Yeah.'

'Bad news that Javel. Now I'm not saying he did it necessarily. Innocent until proven guilty and all that. But regardless he's trouble. And your name has been associated with his quite a bit. Not good that; not good at all.'

'It's not my fault; I didn't do anything wrong.'

'Not entirely true, is it?'

'It is—'

'Enough! He's out the picture now anyway. Up to his neck in trouble.' He looks at me again. 'In future stay away from troublemakers. If you don't, trouble will find you. Got it?'

'Yes.'

There is a bulge in the front pocket of my mini rucksack. It is the drugs. It's all here apart from the ganja which I left at the house. Planning to smoke it with Dougal. Mum's father says, 'Be on your best behaviour for the remainder of your time here.' He takes his left hand off the steering wheel and raises the index finger. 'And in London too. Your mother is going through hell. We all are.' A police pickup truck is racing towards us. Its siren is wailing and the blue light on its roof is flashing. It shoots past and disappears up the road. 'You've told the girl, Dalilah, you're leaving?'

'No, not yet.'

'Because you're planning to tell her in person?'

'Yeah.'

'Break the news gently. And make sure you do it today.'

162

We have arrived. Mum's father goes into the office and speaks with the manager. Behind this washing machine in the corner is the perfect hiding place. I wedge the drugs into the space. Just received a text from Dalilah. She's going to *drop by* later. Three big linen bags crammed with dirty bed linen have been dumped on the bench. Must have been delivered yesterday and the manager couldn't be bothered to unload them into the machines. It will be good riddance to this place. When I come to Antigua on holiday, not going within a hundred metres of a launderette. The first bag smells of piss. Make that two hundred metres. I kick the bag. Then I kick it again. It's not a bag anymore; it's the tourist who pissed on the sheets. *Please no, was an accident.* I bend over and grab him by the collar. Should have rinsed it in water, not left it for me. *I-I forgot.* I say, *No, you didn't forget, the smell of piss would have stopped you forgetting.* I unleash ground and pound. The office door opens and the manager's head appears.

'What's with all the noise?'

'The bags fell on the floor.'

The door closes. I shove the bed linen from the piss bag in a machine, put some detergent and softener in the dispenser, switch it on, and then rinse my hands in the sink. The smell of piss gets me thinking about Javel. Wonder how many times he has pissed his pants in the prison already because he is scared. Lots of times I bet what with all the real gangsters and bad asses who will be bothering him. The office door opens and Mum's father comes out.

'Have a good weekend.'

'You too, Bevis.'

'Work hard, Horatio. See you this evening.'

He leaves … *Beep!* That was a horn. A delivery van has arrived. This job sucks … There are four bags of dirty laundry. Nightmare. I am hauling the last bag up the steps when my phone rings. It's that rich tourist woman's number. I dump the bag on the porch and answer it.

'Hello.'

'Hey, how's things?'

'Not too bad. What're you after?'

'Ah, eight if that's possible. Got a party tonight. Um, can you do that?'

'Yes. Will phone you at five-thirty.'

Will persuade her to take all fifteen grammes off my hands …

Presently, I'm pressing napkins and talking with the manager. She just asked me which is my favourite beach. While folding a napkin I say, 'Best beach I've been to is the one here.'

'The best. Really?'

'Yes, it's got everything. Has a resort at one end with kayak rentals, a bar, and a food van. And it's quiet at the other end. Good transport links too as quite close to the road.'

'You been to Long Bay Beach in the Willikies?'

'No, haven't been to that end of the island.'

'Should check it out before you leave.'

She goes into the office. Dalilah is here. She skips over to me, throws her arms around my neck, and says, 'Surprise.' She whispers in my ear, 'Is she here?'

'Yes.'

'Pity.' She releases her grip on my neck and winks. 'How's everything?'

'Fine.'

'Nothing new to report?'

'I'm leaving.'

'Leaving?'

'Leaving Antigua. Returning to London.'

The corners of Dalilah's mouth curl downwards. She says, 'When?'

'At the end of term.'

She looks up at the ceiling, mutters something, looks at me, and says, 'That's like in a week or two.'

'Yes, final day of term is next Friday. I'm flying the following Monday.'

Mum emailed me yesterday with the flight details. Dalilah's mouth is hanging open. For a while she doesn't say anything. Then she says, 'You're kidding me?'

'I'm not kidding.'

'This c-can't be happening.' She collapses onto the bench and holds her face in her hands. 'Why?'

'Because of my mum. Her sister's ill with cancer and is going to die.'

'*Hhh*, but why do you have to go so soon? You only just moved here.'

'She says I have to return to London to live with her.'

'*H-hhh!*'

She is full-on weeping now. The manager comes out of the office, hurries over to Dalilah, and bends down in front of her.

'*Hhh.*' Dalilah takes her hands off her face. 'He's leaving!'

She covers her face with her hands again. The manager strokes her back. A washing machine has finished its cycle. I go over to it. The manager waddles after me, and whispers, 'What're you doing? Get over there and put your arm around her.'

When I place my left hand on Dalilah's left shoulder, the manager shakes her head. Dalilah lifts her face from her hands. Tears are streaming down her cheeks.

'It's so unfair.'

The manager bends down in front of her again, and says, 'I know, sweetie. But that's the way it's got to be.'

'You knew already!'

'His grandfather just told me. Had an inkling it would be happening, what with his daughter being so ill. Horatio's mother can't very well leave him here indefinitely with his grandfather. Wouldn't be right.'

Dalilah continues crying. Another washing machine's cycle is finished. The laundry needs moving to the drying machines, or it won't be ready in time. I take my hand off Dalilah's shoulder and

165

take a step towards the washing machines. The manager hisses, 'Leave it!'

I step back and put my hand on Dalilah's shoulder again. She is still crying. When she finally stops, she hugs me around my waist and makes whimpering noises. The manager says, 'Don't worry darling he'll be back. He has family out here and he'll be wanting to see you.' She flicks my arm. 'Right?'

'Yeah.'

'See.'

Dalilah peers up at me with wet eyes, and says, 'You promise you'll come back.'

'Yes.'

'Say you promise.'

'I promise.'

While I move laundry to the drying machines, Dalilah sits on the bench. Because she has taken up so much time, my shift is going to overrun. When she goes into the office to talk with the manager, I pull the drugs out from behind the washing machine and stuff them in my mini rucksack. Dalilah comes whimpering out of the office and hugs me tightly around the neck. We organise to meet after school on Tuesday. Then she leaves.

My shift has overrun by seventeen minutes. I text the woman. She texts immediately telling me to come to her house. It is at the far end of the beach near where I met her last time. Meeting at her house is good because this deal might take a while, as I'm planning to negotiate with her. I cross the road and make my way to the beach. It is quite dark by the time I arrive at the villa. There is an illuminated path leading to the front door. I ring the buzzer. My customer opens the front door.

'Come in.'

The villa is open plan, has a wide staircase, the highest ceiling I've ever seen in a house, and a balcony overlooking the ground floor.

'An internal balcony is unusual.'

'It's called a mezzanine.' The floors are white marble, there are ornate vases on plinths, cream-coloured sofas and armchairs, a vast television screen attached to a wall, and two glittering chandeliers. *This woman can't have been in many launderettes.* I follow her into a vast open-plan kitchen. It has marble counters and high-end kitchen utensils. *Even Serena's kitchen isn't this luxurious.* 'You have the stuff?'

I slip the mini rucksack off my back and open it. A man with a shiny black moustache comes in. He looks like an arsehole. He says, 'Hi there. What an amazing sunset, did you see it?'

I say, 'No.'

'The whole sky was orange. There were these incredible clouds and the orange diffused through them.'

'Yeah, it was quite a sight,' says the woman. 'Um, so how much for the eight G's? There's a discount for that much, I'm assuming?'

'No. However, if you buy fifteen I can do a special one-time deal for you. One thousand two hundred. That's eighty per gramme.'

'Eight will do us. Thanks though.'

'Yup,' says the man, 'eight will suffice. Do eight for seven hundred and twenty, and you have a deal.'

'No!'

'What do you mean no?' The man takes a step towards me. 'That's what we're offering.'

'Fifteen for one thousand two hundred, or nothing.'

The man shouts, 'What do you mean by nothing?'

'Exactly that, nothing.'

'You're being too pushy,' he says. 'We're not going to be swayed, so forget it.'

Will just play hardball. They won't be able to get it from anywhere else last minute. Unless they want to risk trying to score on the beach. They will get ripped off.

'Well,' says the woman. 'We have a deal?'

167

'No.'

I stuff the drugs in my mini rucksack and sling it over my shoulder. She shrieks, 'Wait a second!'

I say, 'Deal, or no deal?'

'Deal.'

'Bloody hell,' says the man. 'What sort of service is this? Fucking farce!'

'Calm down, please,' says the woman. 'I'm going to get the money.'

'Whatever,' he says.

She goes upstairs. The man is glaring at me. He says, 'Want to try it before we pay, that's for sure.'

'Go ahead.'

'Taking advantage of customers is wrong. Surely, you must realise it's in your best interests to be reasonable and cordial.' He is smirking. 'Do you even know what cordial means?'

'Means friendly, sociable.'

He mutters something that sounds like *parasite*. He continues glaring at me. He is trying to intimidate me; it's not working though. Right uppercut to the solar plexus, left hook to the liver. And while he's bent over clutching his liver, a right uppercut to the chin. The woman is coming down the stairs.

*

I have just got back to the house and am stuffing the cash in rolled-up socks. Will get all this money changed into pounds in London. Dalilah phones. She tells me how sad she is I am leaving and how unfair it is. She already said that. After the call, I email Serena to tell her I am returning to London. The moment I finish typing the email Mum phones. She has loads to say, none of it interesting.

I am checking the Antiguan news websites to see if there is anything new. There isn't. There will be when Javel gets sentenced to a couple of decades in prison. It will be ages before he goes to court though. The court will be running on Caribbean time. Am downstairs making noodles when there is a knock on the front door. It's Mum's father. He could have just phoned. Is he going to complain I was late getting back. I open the door.

'Good evening.' He slaps me on the shoulder. 'How was work today?'

'Fine.'

'Pleased to hear it. Carlton is having a BBQ. Dougal is there. They're expecting you.' He gives me a plastic bag. There are crisps and a bottle of Coca-Cola in it. 'Your contribution.'

Carlton and Dougal never told me about the BBQ. They could have sent me a text. I put on some mosquito spray, take some of the ganja I took from the dealer, and go over to Carlton's. They are both on the porch. Dougal is drinking a bottle of beer and Carlton is cooking chicken on a grill. Carlton says, 'Evening.'

Dougal says, 'Wah gwaan, Cuz?' I give Carlton the bag with the crisps and the Coca-Cola in it, and then ask Dougal if he wants to smoke. He says he does. We perch on the edge of the porch. I pass the ganja to him. He smells it and rotates it in his fingertips. 'Top quality import dis. Fair bit here too.' He looks at me. 'Must have cost you a fair few EC.' Dougal pulls a cigarette paper from a packet and breaks off a piece of ganja. 'Caught de murderer, I hear. Was dat claffy who burnt de launderette. Farm fool.'

'Javel.'

'Right, Javel ...' He sparks the spliff, inhales on it, and exhales. 'Was a drug dealer who was murdered.'

'Yes.'

'Mmm.'

He passes me the spliff. I have some puffs on it. Dougal is watching me out of the corner of his eye. The chicken is ready. I get a piece, some rice and salad, and sit on a chair on the porch. Dougal and Carlton have moved to the far end of the porch. They must be talking quietly, as can't hear what they are saying from here. They are both looking at me. Carlton is shaking his head; Dougal is sucking on his lower lip. I say, 'This chicken is good.'

*

The following Friday – It's the last day of term, and I am in the last class of the day, English. My final class at this school. For the most part this school is okay. It's small and the facilities suck, but the teaching isn't bad on the whole, and the boys are well behaved. I have just completed a written test on *Jane Eyre*. Was easy, could have done it in my sleep. The teacher collects the test papers off the desks, goes to the front of the class, and says, 'As you all know, our resident *Jane Eyre* expert is leaving us. He is returning to the UK. Horatio, wherever you end up at school next, you will thrive academically. I'm quite sure of it. That's it for this term. Enjoy your holidays and make sure you do the reading that's been set.'

On my way out of the classroom, the teacher shakes my hand. In the corridor Ezequiel says to me, 'Why did you bother with the hassle of moving to a new school for just one term?'

'My mother's idea, not mine. She's returned to London and wants me there.'

'Sounds like a lot of upheaval to me.'

Outside the school gates, Garfield slaps me on the shoulder, and says, 'You're super smart and you've got some bowling skills. Good luck.'

He shakes my hand. I walk to the bus stop with some of the boys. Cornelius says, 'Your time on the island was short and sweet.' He offers me chewing gum. I take a piece. 'When you come here on holiday, we'll practice in the nets. Will be like old times.'

'Yeah, we'll do that.'

The bus is here. Stopping off on the way to have a walk on the beach with Dalilah.

170

TWELVE

MY FLIGHT TO HEATHROW is with British Airways at 19:23. Now for a final check of my room. There is nothing in the bathroom, nothing in the chest of drawers, nothing under the bed, nothing on the bed. Everything is packed in my suitcase and mini rucksack. The money is stashed in my suitcase. I sling the mini rucksack over my shoulder, pick up the suitcase by its handle and haul it downstairs. There is nothing of mine down here other than my baseball cap, which I put it on. I open the door and go outside with my luggage. They are all in the courtyard watching me. Carlton's daughter waves at me, and shrieks, 'Bye bye.'

Carlton shakes my hand, and says, 'Goodbye and good luck.'

Dougal says in a quiet voice, 'You haven't changed a bit, Cuz. Still de same as when you were little. A liability.'

Genevieve marches over to me, and says, 'Listen boy. If you don't allow space for The Lord in your heart, there is no saving you.' She prods me in the chest. 'We have taken you to church, but your eyes don't see The Lord, your ears don't hear The Lord, and your mouth is mute to The Lord—'

'That's enough, darling,' says Mum's father.

'The Lord is your only salvation. Without The Lord you will remain a lost soul forever.' She marches off. 'May The Lord have mercy on you.'

Nightmare she is. I carry my luggage out of the courtyard and put it in the boot of the Toyota. I get in the front passenger seat. Mum's father gets in the driver seat and sticks the key in the ignition. We drive off. He looks in both directions and turns onto the main road. I text Dalilah to say I've just left.

'Sorry about Genevieve. She can get a little carried away sometimes. But it's because she wants the best for you. We all do.' He glances at me. 'Got everything a boy could want. Brains, looks, athleticism. If you can get your behaviour up to the standard of your schoolwork, there'll be no stopping you.' *Wonder what films they will have on the plane. Must be one or two worth watching.* I look out of the window. He doesn't say anything for a while. Getting close to the launderette when he says, 'Hard for her you leaving. You know that, right?'

'Yeah.'

'Give her a nice goodbye.'

Dalilah is waiting on the corner by the launderette. When I get out of the car, she rushes over to me and wraps her arms around my neck. She is standing on tiptoes and her damp cheek is pressed to mine.

'I'll miss you so much.' She continues gripping onto my neck. '*H-hh* when will you come and visit me?'

'Will come here on holiday at some point. Won't be for a while.'

'How long's a while?'

Who knows? Mum's father leans out of the window, and says, 'Don't worry darling, he has family here and will return.'

She is still gripping onto my neck and making whimpering noises. Mum's father says, 'We best get going, traffic could be bad.'

Dalilah kisses me on the lips and slowly releases her grip. I say 'Goodbye,' and get into the car.

When we drive off, she waves with both hands. Mum's father *tuts* and says, 'Wave.'

172

I extend my arm through the open window and move it up and down. Saturday was my last shift at the launderette. Only worked the morning. In the afternoon went kayaking with Dalilah, ate ice cream at the food van, and had sex at her house. Her mother was out. He is talking about Mum and how difficult it is for her with her sister in hospital with no hope of recovery. The traffic is slowing down. It's because of the roadworks.

Finally, we are at the airport. He takes my suitcase from the boot; I take the mini rucksack. He drags the suitcase towards the terminal building. On the way he says, 'Don't forget your mother needs support right now. She's going through hell and is going to be stressed.' He stops outside the terminal's electronic door. 'Will be coming to London in a month or a two. All depends on what's happening with Tanice.' He blows air from his mouth. 'Sorry things didn't work out over here as planned. Not easy moving to a new country, starting a new school, and then having to leave right away. But that's the way things go sometimes.' He grips my left shoulder with his right hand. 'Have a nice flight. Bye for now.'

'Goodbye.'

I drag the suitcase into the terminal building and join the queue for check-in. Can hear electronic keyboard music coming from the floor above. It is the same sort of music that was being played when I arrived in Antigua.

*

Two days later – I have just left a tube station and am walking along the pavement with Mum. We are going to the hospital. In my mini rucksack is a stack of Eastern Caribbean dollars and my passport. After the hospital I am visiting Serena. On the way to Aunt Fatso's flat, I will stop off at a bureau de change and get the money changed into pounds. Mum is nibbling on the nail of her right thumb. She stops doing it and says, 'Remember what I told you. Be upbeat, tell her you're happy to see her, and you had a

173

good time in Antigua. You can talk about what you enjoyed doing over there. Seeing family, playing cricket. Didn't you go kayaking?'

'Yeah.'

'It's clear what's expected of you, then ...? Horatio!'

'Yes.'

We go into the hospital and get in a lift. We get out of the lift and walk along a corridor. Mum speaks to a nurse. The nurse knocks on a door, opens it slightly, and says, 'Tanice, you have visitors.'

We enter the room. Mum says, 'Afternoon Sis. Look who's come to see you.'

She is lying on her back in bed. Her face is a sort of grey colour and her cheeks are sunken. Before they were fat like a hamster's. I say, 'Hello.'

She murmurs, 'Hey.'

Either the food sucks here, or cancer has stopped her craving food bigtime. Mum nudges me with her elbow. She wants me to say I'm happy to see her. No way, I'm not going to lie. She nudges me again. I say, 'Antigua was fun. Well, some of it was anyway. I went kayaking, played cricket, did some other stuff.'

Aunt Fatso murmurs something. Mum places her hand on my arm – 'He found a nice girlfriend there I'm told. Dad says she is incredibly pretty.' Aunt Fatso blinks. Mum bends forward and grasps her hand. 'How're you feeling today?'

'Pretty jaded.'

'How is the new medication working out?'

'Hard to say. No change really ...'

Her voice is weak and much less bossy than before. While they talk, I inspect the room. It's tiny and practically half the space is taken up by the bed. Usually, Aunt Fatso is surrounded by chocolate. But I can't see any. Behind me is the only other bit of furniture in here – a thin table on wheels. And there's chocolate on it. A red carton of Lindt Lindor milk chocolate truffles. The

174

carton is open, but hardly any of the chocolate truffles have been eaten. Mum says, 'What're you looking over there for?' I swivel around. 'Going to have a quick word with the doctor. You stay here and tell Tanice more about Antigua.'

Mum nudges me with her elbow. I say, 'My school was by the cathedral in St. John's. It was boys only.' Mum is nodding. 'It didn't have much in the way of facilities. The teaching on the whole was pretty decent though …'

Mum exits the room and closes the door behind her. I stop talking. Aunt Fatso doesn't say anything and nor do I. The only sound in here is the ticking of an alarm clock on the table next to the Lindt chocolate truffles. She blinks twice. Someone is coughing in the corridor. Aunt Fatso has closed her eyes. Wonder what Lindt chocolate truffles taste like, I've never tried them before. I take one from the box, unwrap it and put it in my mouth. Tastes rich and quite sickly. As Aunt Fatso knows full well, Maltesers, M&M's etc. can be scoffed all day long. But scoffing Lindt chocolate truffles could result in puking. That wouldn't have stopped her from having a good go. Her eyes are still closed. I take another chocolate truffle from the box and put it in my mouth. Mum comes in. I swallow.

'Had a quick chat with the doctor. She's going to drop by in a bit to see how you're doing.' Aunt Fatso opens her eyes. 'You two have a nice chat?' I don't say anything and neither does she. 'Horatio is off to see his friend, Serena.' Mum is looking at me. 'You know how to get there; we went through it. It's the Falton Road stop after the park.'

'I know.'

'Be back by eight. Say goodbye to your aunt then.'

'Goodbye.'

Aunt Fatso doesn't say anything. Mum says, 'You'll see him soon.'

I leave. It's annoying as Serena only lives a twenty-minute walk from Aunt Fatso's flat. Because I came to the hospital, am now much further away. I don't have to wait long for the bus. It's pretty rammed but I find a seat on the top deck. I look out of the window. It's a grey day, has been raining on and off. The pavement is heaving with people, the road heaving with traffic. A flock of motley-coloured pigeons land on the pavement and peck at rubbish.

My phone *beeps*. It's a text from Serena saying she'll meet me at the bus stop near her house. I text her – *ETA 7 mins approx.* I keep looking out the window. The traffic is moving quicker … There she is, waiting at the bus stop. Long, silky blonde hair, pink spandex leggings, and a fluffy white sweater. Probably cashmere. When I get off the bus she shrieks, races over to me and hugs me.

'Haven't seen you in ages.' She holds her hands at her sides at shoulder height with the palms turned upwards. 'How do I look?'

'Hot.'

'Oh, thank you.' She lowers her hands. 'Dressed like this cos been at netball. You've grown a bit I think.' She wraps her arm around mine. We cross the road. 'What's it like being back in rainy, grey London? Sucks right, apart from being with me of course.'

'Yeah, pretty much.'

When we arrive at the house, Serena's mother says, 'Horatio *hi*. How was Antigua?'

'Was alright. Weather was good and my school was okay.'

'Fantastic. Serena is so pleased your back.'

'*Mum!* Don't embarrass me.'

'Wasn't. I was just saying. Horatio, would you like a drink? We have Pepsi.'

'Yes please.' We go into the kitchen. Her mother gives me a can of Pepsi and a glass. 'Thank you.'

I follow Serena up the stairs. Her mother shouts, 'Serena, where are you going?'

'My room. Where else?'

'No, want you two down here.'

'Whatever.' We go into the living room. 'So annoying my mum.' Serena plunks herself on the sofa. I sit next to her. 'Did you do anything cool before you left Antigua? And don't say school, launderette, or rotting body.'

'Went to the beach and went kayaking.' I lower my voice. 'Smoked pot with my cousin Dougal.'

'Dougal! What kind of name is that …? So, you've swapped crack for weed. I've started smoking it too, weed that is … Going to Singapore tomorrow and I haven't even packed.' We talk for a while. 'Want to play PlayStation?'

'Sure. Do you still have *Spider-Man*?'

'Sold it. Don't have that dancing game either we used to play. Lent it to someone.'

'*Call of Duty*?'

'No, can't stand war games, they're for boys.' She gets up off the sofa and picks up a PlayStation game in each hand. '*Fortnite* or *Gran Turismo 7*?'

'*Gran Turismo*.'

'Only played it like twice. It's my friend's game.' She inserts the game into the PlayStation … *Realistic this driving game.* I swerve around a corner and hit the accelerator. Serena is lagging way behind. 'If I can't even drive in a computer game, how am I ever going to pass my driving test?'

'Good question.'

She slaps me on the knee, and says, 'Not the answer I was looking for.' After the game we sit on the sofa and chat. Serena flicks a strand of silky blonde hair off her face. 'We're not kids anymore, I'll be sixteen soon.' She flicks another strand of hair off her face and strokes my thigh with her fingertips. 'Missed you loads.'

Her mother comes into the room. Serena *huffs*, and her mother says, 'How are you two getting on?'

An hour later – I say goodbye to Serena and her mother, go to the bus stop, and get on a bus. Getting off at the second stop to go

177

to a bureau de change I found on the internet. The traffic is bad. There's a text from Mum, asking how I'm getting on. I reply, *Fine* … I get off the bus. This street is full of shabby people – tramps and refugee types. The bureau de change is just a grimy window with a grumpy woman behind it with bloated cheeks. She looks a bit like Aunt Fatso used to. I get the money and my passport from my mini rucksack. Changing two hundred pounds worth of Eastern Caribbean Dollars today. Don't want to do it all at once, as the bureau de change might get suspicious where the money came from because I'm young. Hamster Cheeks checks my passport, counts the money, and passes me two hundred and three pounds and sixty-three pence. I put the money in my mini rucksack and walk off.

Am about twenty metres from the bus stop when I see a man slinking out of a pawnbrokers. He's dirty looking, tall, skinny, has a small head, and a really long nose. *Rat!* Mum's dead boyfriend's best friend. Only friend. *Ha*, the one I got arrested at the cemetery after his funeral. I planted erotic asphyxiation paraphernalia in his bag and phoned the police. That was the last time I saw him.

'OI!' Rat has seen me. He is coming this way. I walk quickly to the bus stop. The bus is coming. Rat barges past some people and grabs the collar of my jacket. 'Horatio! I went down for what you did.' He tugs my collar. 'You killed my best friend.' The bus is here. I will hit him and get on it. 'Yeah, know you killed Brandon, you sick fuck!' I hit him with a left hook to the side of his head. '*Mahh.*' He drops to one knee. I squirm through the queuing people, board the bus, and press my bankcard to the reader. Rat is on his feet. He barges someone out of the way and steps onto the bus. The driver shouts, 'Off my bus!'

'Nah, not till that cunt over there gets off!' He is pointing at me. A man on the pavement pulls the back of Rat's jacket and he topples off the bus. The doors close. Rat is smacking the window. 'I'll kill you!' The bus is moving. 'YOU'RE DEAD! *DEAD!*'

The passengers are looking out of the windows at Rat. *Ha,*

what an idiot. I go to the upper deck to get a better view. I can see him through the rear window. He is chasing the bus and shaking his fists in the air. Hilarious. This is almost as funny as when I got him arrested. Rat said he went down for it.

'HA, HA HAHA ...'

He is still chasing the bus. I am laughing so much my eyes are watering and my sides hurt. The bus has stopped.

'Get off my bus!'

The driver is standing over me. I wipe my eyes with my sleeve and look out of the rear window. Rat has disappeared. Will walk the rest of the way; it's not that far from here. Everyone stares at me as I make my way to the stairs. Have just stepped off the bus when I hear shouting. It's Rat. He is charging along the pavement towards me.

'DEVIL CUNT!'

To be continued …

Please leave a review for Arcadia. Reviews are vital to us authors for finding new readers.

Printed in Great Britain
by Amazon